WHAT IS MINE

José Henrique Bortoluci was born in Jaú in 1984. He has a BA in International Relations and an MA in Social History from the University of São Paulo, as well as an MA and a PhD in Sociology from the University of Michigan, where he lectured and was a Fulbright fellow. He is a professor of sociology at the Fundação Getúlio Vargas in São Paulo, where his lectures and research revolve around Brazilian politics, social theory, democracy and social movements.

Rahul Bery is based in Cardiff, Wales, and translates from Spanish and Portuguese to English. His published translations include novels by Vicente Luis Mora, Afonso Cruz, Simone Campos and David Trueba.

'Powerful in its atomization of the Brazilian style of "capitalist devastation" that goes by the name of progress, movingly tender in its evocation of an Odysseus of a father, a long-distance trucker who plays a part in the construction of the Trans-Amazonian Highway, this is a memoir like no other. I read it in one great gulp, unable to put it down. Brilliant!'
—— Lisa Appignanesi, author of *Everyday Madness*

'A political document told as memoir, this is a book of incredible beauty and insight, one which demonstrates one of the greatest truths: that our lives, and the lives of our families, are inextricably bound to the structures of class, economics, and history they were born into.'
—— Madeleine Watts, author of *The Inland Sea*

'*What Is Mine* is an unforgettable oral history of truck driving along the potholed roads carving up the Amazon rainforest: bandits, sleep deprivation, beef barbecued on the engine. It is also an incisive political critique of ecocidal ideas of "progress", a powerful reflection on the ways labour shapes a human body, and a loving exploration of a relationship between a father and son. It already has the feel of a classic.'
—— Caleb Klaces, author of *Fatherhood*

'José Henrique Bortoluci's *What Is Mine* is an extraordinarily powerful portrait of a man's life, a country's course and the "ancient marriage between shamelessness and devastation" in Brazilian history. Tender, thought-provoking, incisive and humane, it's a deeply intelligent road movie for the soul. A beautiful and moving journey through a trucker's memories of a changing nation and a vital meditation on class, capitalism and, above all else, the search for human dignity. Utterly transfixing.'
—— Julian Hoffman, author of *Irreplaceable*

Fitzcarraldo Editions

WHAT IS MINE

JOSÉ HENRIQUE BORTOLUCI

Translated by

RAHUL BERY

CONTENTS

I. REMEMBER AND TELL MY STORY 11

II. NOW YOU KNOW 33

III. URGE TO SEE 53

IV. NESTOR 77

V. KILLING AND KILLING 81

VI. MANELÃO 103

VII. THESE PEOPLE 107

VIII. JAQUES 119

IX. CAB 125

X. WHAT IS MINE 133

'There's no text without filiation.'
—— Roland Barthes

'In any case, we desire a miracle of eight
million kilometres for Brazil.'
—— Graciliano Ramos

I. REMEMBER AND TELL MY STORY

'My father always away and his absence always with me. And the river, always the river, perpetually renewing itself.'
— João Guimarães Rosa, 'The Third Bank of the River'

Remember, your dad helped build this airport so you could fly. I hear my father's words every time I catch a flight from Guarulhos Airport. And while I always remembered, it has taken me some time to truly understand. The truck driver father visits his home, his wife and his kids. He comes and, before long, leaves again. He always came with his truck, they were a duo, almost a single entity, both too much and not enough, imposing and ephemeral. As a boy, I always wanted them to stay, wanted them to go, wanted to go with them.

He said these exact words when we were on our way to that airport in 2009, the day I left to do my PhD in Sociology in the United States. During the months I spent preparing for the move, I showed him the state of Michigan several times on the map. We calculated the distance between Jaú and Ann Arbor, where I would live for the next six years. My father doesn't understand the world of universities, is unfamiliar with its nomenclature and rituals. He has only a vague notion of what it means to do a PhD. But he does understand distances.

Eight thousand kilometres separate the two cities. This number failed to impress him. He had covered hundreds of times that distance over five decades as a truck driver. One day he asked me to calculate how many times you could travel around the world with the distance he had covered as a driver.

Could it get you to the moon?

In my father's imagination, a journey from Earth to the moon is a more solid concept than my life as an academic, teacher and writer.

Words are roads. They're what we use to connect the dots between the present and a past we no longer have access to.

Words are scars, the remnants of our experiences of cutting and sewing up the world, gathering its pieces, tying back together the things that had the temerity to scatter.

Words were the world my father brought with him in his truck during my childhood. They resounded by themselves – *cabin, Trans-Amazonian, trailer, highway, Pororoca, Belém, homesickness* – or formed part of narratives about a world that seemed impossibly large. I had to imagine them in all their colours, record them in my memory and cling onto them, because soon my father would leave and he wouldn't be back for forty or fifty days.

Most of these stories were reconstructions of events he had witnessed or heard about on the road. Others were fantastical creations: the epic hunt for a giant bird in Amazonia, the fable of a sheep he found on the highway and took on as his cabin companion, journeys over the Bolivian border with groups of hippies in the 1970s. Many, I imagine, mixed fact and fantasy. He described in detail seeing UFOs on a highway in Mato Grosso, nights spent in isolated indigenous villages, brawls with armed soldiers, Homeric rescues of trucks that had fallen into ravines.

—

His name is José Bortoluci. At home, everyone calls him Didi, but on the road he was always Jaú. The fifth child in a family of nine siblings, he was born in December 1943, in the rural part of that city located in the interior of São Paulo state.

My father studied until he was nine, worked on the family's small farm from the age of seven, moved with them to the city at fifteen. He was only twenty-two when he became a truck driver. *I was young, but I was as brave as a lion.* He started driving trucks in 1965 and retired in 2015. The country that he traversed and helped to build was very different then from how it is now, but in recent years there has been a sense of familiarity: a country seized by frontier logic, the principle of expansion at any cost, the 'colonization' of new territories, environmental vandalism, the slow and clumsy construction of an ever more unequal consumer society. Roads and trucks occupy a key position in this fantasy of a developed nation in which forests and rivers give way to highways, prospecting, pasture and factories.

The truck would bring my father, his dirty clothes and not enough money. My mother would agonize and work overtime altering clothes while looking after her two sons.

I am the oldest son. I understood from very early on that our family life was overshadowed by the risk of extreme poverty, uncontrolled inflation and premature illness.

We got used to living in a state of uncertainty, at the mercy of bank accounts that were on the brink of collapse, and with strict limits on what we could eat, experience, wish for. We never went hungry, though at times this was only thanks to help from neighbours, friends and relatives when my family's income ran out and my father's debts were at their peak. I do, however, remember growing accustomed to that 'half-starvation you feel at the smell of dinner coming from the doors of the more well-to-do', as the Danish poet Tove Ditlevsen described it in her memoirs. A persistent semi-starvation which we learnt to downplay, misleadingly labelling it as 'cravings'. In my case, the sensation was further incited by the adverts for sweet yoghurts and cereals that flooded TVs in the 1980s and 1990s and which, to this day, provoke an uncomfortable temptation in me, emerging like a discordant echo of past desires.

A good proportion of the clothes my brother and I wore during the first twenty years of our lives had been bought second-hand, donated by an uncle or aunt or some family friends, or purchased at charity jumble sales. My mother, whose work as a seamstress helped with household expenses, always made a point of keeping them impeccably clean and repairing any blemishes. The newer ones were 'church clothes', the older ones for wearing on weekdays.

Our house was small and stuffy, built bit by bit at the rear of my grandparents' house. The uncovered kitchen flooded at the first sign of heavy rain. This was the room where my brother and I studied after school and where my mother worked all day. The soundtrack to our lives was composed of the noise from her sewing machine and the songs on the radio, tuned in to some local station. Endless work, little money, and no time to undo what had been woven: there is no Ulysses, no Penelope in this story.

My mother hated him smoking inside the house. So, whenever he was in Jaú, my father spent a lot of time sitting on a step between the kitchen and the small yard connecting our home to my grandparents' house. That step, the threshold between inside and out, made concrete the uncertain status that my father occupied for me, a man who was both an essential part of my life and a seasonal visitor who disrupted the rhythm of our days.

There were always bills to pay. A silent terror associated with the expression 'overdraft', which I must have learnt in my earliest years, always hung in the ether at home. And which clung, most of all, to the word 'debt': a suffocating word which spread through the rooms like cigarette smoke. That word arrived with the truck and stayed even after my father had left. To this day, hearing someone say 'debt' brings to mind the smell of cigarettes and the image of that step in my childhood home.

There is almost no written record of his fifty years on the road – just two postcards sent to my mother and some yellowing invoices in the drawer. But he remembers a lot, and his 'madeleines' emerge when you least expect it: an image on TV makes him remember when he went for several days without food, stuck on a muddy track in southern Pará; any news of a serious accident on the road opens up a whole trove of stories about the many he witnessed and the handful he was involved in; stories of remote villages, of poachers, of distant tropical landscapes, of companions – some loyal, others not, most of them dead. Narratives that march along and spring back to life without the help of photos or notes. The only thing anchoring them is the memory of a man who is nearly eighty, now somewhat garbled by time.

I've seen so many things, son. I should've written them down, taken photos. We didn't have mobiles or anything like that back then. They didn't exist. The only thing I could've taken them with would have been a Kodak, those black and white

cameras, but your old man never had one. Because if I did have
a record of all the things I've done you'd be so proud of your dad.
It may seem like I don't have much to show for it, but what is
mine is everything I saw and recorded in my memory. So all I
can do is try to remember and tell my story.

Photos showing my father on his travels during this
five-decade period are also few and far between. Most of
the ones that do exist record his presence on commem-
orative dates, when he was with his family in Jaú.

In one of those images, the two of us are in our kitchen
at home. It's my first birthday in November 1985. He is
holding me up in the air while my cousins sing 'Happy
Birthday' around the cake. The scene is made up of colourful balloons, blue plastic cups and a large glass bottle
of Coca-Cola. His hands hold me tight and I appear con-
fident; my body is erect, with only the tips of my toes,
inside my tiny red plimsolls, brushing against the table.
I'm looking at the camera, my eyes open and alert, while
he looks at me. My hair was fairer than it is today and his
hadn't yet lost its colour; it's combed backwards, long,
shiny and slathered with Trim, the styling cream he used
for decades, until recently he decided he wouldn't use it
any more and would keep his hair short – the same hair-
cut my grandfather had in his old age. My small, white
hands rest on my father's heavily sunburnt skin, distin-
guished by an uneven tan, typical of truck drivers, which
he still has to this day, though now his skin is discoloured
and speckled with blotches and scars. One small hand
on his arm, another on the fingers of one of the hands
holding me. This is one of the only photographs in which
my mother does not appear (did she take it?).

A couple of days after the party, my father would go
back on the road before returning to Jaú a few weeks later,

for Christmas maybe, or for the birth of my brother six weeks after. In a journal that my mother kept for years, from the beginning of her relationship with my father in 1976 until shortly after my birth, she describes this time, stretched out by distance: 'How I love you Didi, I'd repeat these words a million times if you were right here by my side all day. But I know that's impossible because I have to work and so do you, so that we can achieve our dream. Distance creates longing, but never forgetting.'

I don't know what the dream she talks about is or if, now, she believes she has achieved it. This entry is dated 3 June 1976, but the tone used in these lines is repeated dozens of times in the pages of her journal over the nine years that follow.

Isolated at home because of the collapse of the health system in the Jaú region, one of the worst affected by the coronavirus during those sorrowful early days of 2021, my father looked animated as he told his stories. I began recording them in January of that year, during successive visits to my parents, always on warm nights after dinner. He preferred to talk to me in the backyard, lying in an old hammock he'd bought in the 1970s in some city in Piauí, which accompanied him on his travels for years.

This conversation we're having right now, son, you'll have to keep it in your memory, because you know your dad won't be around for long.

After one of these recording sessions, he wondered out loud if he would live to see the book published. I had been wondering the same thing since December 2020, when he told me for the first time about the strange abdominal pains he was having and the blood that had been appearing in his faeces for several weeks.

As I write these lines, in early 2021, my father, at seventy-eight, is beginning treatment for bowel cancer. The tumour emerged in his body before spreading throughout our family life and into this book.

The cancer was diagnosed on 29 December 2020, before I began a series of interviews with him, but after I'd told him I wanted to record our conversations, hear him talk about the road, the story of his life, his 'yarns', memories and anything else he wanted to say.

The first time I told him I was writing a book, he asked if it would be a good thing for me. Yes, I answered, I think so. *If it's good for you, then I'm happy.*

The day before the diagnosis, I was in São Paulo and had spent the whole afternoon staring at maps of Amazonian rivers and the roads of the north of the country. I read about periods of flooding and dry spells, about the most suitable times for visiting river beaches, navigating the smaller streams and observing the surrounding jungle. I started planning a journey across the entire Trans-Amazonian Highway (how would I manage when I can't even drive?). I ordered three maps of the region, the huge ones that you have to fold and unfold, as well as detailed road maps which showed the smaller roads that cut through the rainforest, those asphalt anti-rivers my father helped build in the region he traversed for decades.

That same night, a pipe burst in my apartment. The water flooded the entire bathroom, part of the kitchen, the utility room and the entrance hallway before leaking out of the apartment. This attracted the attention of the building's concierge, who called me, concerned. I was out but managed to get back quickly. The living room was the worst hit, completely covered by a thick layer of liquid, a foot of water on the wooden floor, like a gently oscillating mirror, reflecting lampshades, armchairs, plants and the image of my own body. That small apartment in the centre of São Paulo with its modern furniture, which had finally allowed me to create something resembling a middle-class adult home – so different from the house I grew up in – had been brought down by water that came up to my shins.

I felt jittery and fearful. The out-of-place water felt too theatrical, an ill omen, as if it had come straight out of one of Marguerite Duras's colonial novels or a surrealist painting. The water had soaked my shoes, the hem of my trousers, pillows, wooden furniture, and was seeping into thousands of tiny cracks in the floor tiles, warping them forever. In my room, the cat was hiding under the bed, one of the few places untouched by the water.

There's a sense of overflow with cancer too: it's matter in the wrong place, in frenetic expansion.

I called Jaú the following morning and asked my mother what the diagnosis was from the bowel biopsy they had taken at the laboratory. She struggled to pronounce the strange word. She decided to spell it out and I wrote it down on a piece of paper: a-d-e-n-o-c-a-r-c-i-n-o-m-a. Letter by letter the word formed, each letter a cell joining onto others to form a new meaning, an out-of-place word-mass.

A rapid Google search explained that 'adenocarcinoma' is the medical term for a certain kind of tumour that affects epithelial glandular tissues, such as those in the rectum, as was my father's case. This was the first of many words to enter our growing family lexicon over the months to come. Illness is not simply a biological phenomenon, but also heralds a new kingdom of words, a mesh of vocabulary that colonizes our everyday language.

We have all experienced this in recent years, when the coronavirus forced us to dive into a terminological lake of 'moving averages', 'protein spikes', 'herd immunity', 'immunity window' and so on. In my family's case, we were also surrounded by words in rapid proliferation that began to circulate around my father's body, connecting to it and altering its dimensions.

After that inaugural period, other words and expressions piled up: 'stoma', 'colostomy', 'tumour markers', 'PET scan', 'colorectal tumour'. And 'malignant neoplasia', the cruellest of all, perhaps because it suggests a kind of moral drama, perhaps because it is the most honest.

In the first medical consultations, I quickly learn that the taboo surrounding the word 'cancer' isn't restricted to the world of patients and their family members. A careful observer would have to go to some lengths to find it mentioned in reports, exams, hospital routines, conversations with doctors and nurses. We still describe cancer patients as 'battling a disease', and you don't have to have been around for long to realize that the 'disease' being battled is never flu, cholera or pneumonia. Its absence seems to make it more alive – in this silence, we all know it's cancer that's being talked about.

Susan Sontag famously wrote that '[e]veryone who is born holds dual citizenship, in the kingdom of the well and in the kingdom of the sick. Although we all prefer to use only the good passport, sooner or later each of us is obliged, at least for a spell, to identify ourselves as citizens of that other place.' The American writer was very familiar with this condition of double belonging; she faced a series of relapses, and ensuing cancer treatment, over the last thirty years of her life.

My father travels with this new passport. The imprints

he now bears and the rituals to which he is subjected – the perennial colostomy bag, the intermittent urinary catheter, the frequent hospital visits, the operations – all signal his citizenship of the world of the sick.

In a well known piece of dialogue in Ernest Hemingway's novel *The Sun Also Rises*, a war veteran and bankrupt former millionaire explains to a colleague how his economic ruin came to pass:
  "'How did you go bankrupt?"
  "Two ways. Gradually and then suddenly."'
  Observing my father over the last few years, I have learnt that growing old also obeys this double rhythm. You grow old gradually: muscles lose their strength, new pains emerge in the body, cataracts cloud your vision, your hearing stops catching nuances, familiar stairs become Olympic-level obstacles; surgery, hospital stays and the deaths of acquaintances begin to dominate conversations with friends and relatives of the same age.
  You also grow old suddenly. My father's great leap came with the diagnosis of bowel cancer and the treatment that followed.
  Life passes quickly after forty, but it's been flying by since I found out about the illness.
  'Severe heart disease', the patient records state; 'Your father is a complicated patient,' the doctors who see him say; 'We have fewer treatment options with you, sir,' the oncologist repeats at every consultation.
  Memories emerge and intertwine: he remembers that his father and two of his brothers died of bowel cancer. *My grandma Maria had it too. She had surgery on her tumour the day Brasília was inaugurated. She lived a good while after though, I don't think it's what killed her.*
  The fragile condition of his heart means the doctors

cannot carry out the extensive surgery to remove the tumour. Or at least that's what the first surgeon concluded, but we're rarely fully convinced by the medical pathways set out before us. Where health is concerned, doubt becomes a permanent condition. We never felt persuaded they couldn't operate and remove the tumour, while also being terrified this was indeed the case.

I write between two devastations. One of them afflicts my father's body. The other is collective, national. In recent years we have been laid to waste by a macabre political experiment: the great evil that did nothing but bare its teeth at the growing pile of dead bodies we've long ago given up trying to keep count of.

Just as our bodies and fortunes enter a crisis in the double rhythm of the gradual and the sudden, so, too, can countries be devastated at a similar pace. It's undeniable that Brazil's current crisis is just another chapter in its long history of violence. But our collective sickness also suddenly became material in October 2018, when the embodiment of our barbarism was elected to occupy the highest post in the Republic.

A few months earlier, over the course of ten days in May of that year, the nation had been stunned by the mysterious standstill of truck drivers across the entire country. Those workers of the highways erupted like an uncomfortable spectre into the country's political arena. Since then, 'truck drivers' have become indeterminate individuals, keeping a watchful eye on the Brazilian imagination, terrifying the politicians of the moment and exciting opportunistic leaders eager to hijack the political power of those workers by threatening a return to the strikes of 2018.

My father's body, which was already crisscrossed with scars, has gained even more since the diagnosis in December 2020. He entered a foreign territory, and we accompanied him closely, like travellers without a map, asking for directions along the way and orienting themselves through intuition or from the memory of other journeys.

A colostomy bag was connected to the left side of his body in April 2021. It must be emptied several times a day and changed weekly. These bags will accompany him for the rest of his life, gathering the excrement eliminated by a stoma, a kind of anus without a sphincter, surgically constructed by the diversion from the intestine to the surface of the abdomen. Then there would be several radiotherapy sessions and an alarming succession of consultations, examinations and hospital stays, always preceded by countless hours spent in packed waiting rooms.

Shortly after the colostomy surgery, he stops urinating because his prostate has grown unusually large, which means he needs to have a catheter that accompanies him for three months, until another surgical procedure – a 'prostate scraping' – partially restores this basic physiological capacity to him, at least for a time. The stoma works well and he gets used to the unpleasant rituals of maintenance and cleaning, but then a hernia grows uncontrollably around it. The immense protuberance is uncomfortable, deforming his body and forcing him to continually wear a wide and tight-fitting belt.

Time begins to move to the rhythm of the constant wait for the next set of results. We are engulfed by the fear of possible future surgery, by the worsening of his heart condition, by the dread of receiving news of new tumours.

We hear the words 'nodule' and 'lung' together for the first time in February 2022, when another medical speciality, pneumology, is called upon to take part in this long scrutiny of his body. It left the stage the way it entered, one month and several examinations later, when the doctors concluded that it 'probably' wasn't a new tumour. No, there was no need to talk about metastasis, at least not yet.

How do you narrate the life of an ordinary man? I'm hindered by the silence of the sources, the erasure of any records of the people who build the world, who write their stories with hands and feet, with words that are spoken and sung, with sweat and blemished skin. I try to enter the territory of the constant coming and going of those who hardly ever took photos, or wrote journals, or gave interviews, or were filmed. I searched, as Bertolt Brecht suggests we do, for the ones who build the palaces and the walls, not the nobles and generals who command them; the cooks, drivers, gardeners and cleaners, not the dignitaries in the halls of power.

Forgotten heroes. After fifty years driving a truck, I can say this with certainty: we truck drivers are forgotten heroes. We're mistreated, people look down on us. You're the only one who hasn't forgotten me, son. No one values my work, no one. They don't see how much we suffer, having to get up at two in the morning, driving till eleven-thirty, midnight, going without food, risking death in an accident or being robbed, the difficulty of being away from your family.

I like hearing him talk about the day-to-day, about the sensations and small memories that mark out the rhythm of life: 'mundane feelings, thoughts and words. I am trying to capture the life of the soul,' as Svetlana Alexievich writes. I often catch myself trying to find out details about the stops along his routes, where he ate or washed, what he smelt, the people he spoke to. The things he saw and tells me about, the things he will never tell me, the things he merely suggests, the things already lost in time, the things entirely reconstructed by memory.

From the outset, I tried not to be guided by my academic training and produce a social history of Brazilian truck drivers, or a historical sociology of a professional category in which my father would be a 'case study'.

Nor is this a biography. Despite my curiosity, this is not about 'setting the record straight' or giving precise information about the places he visited, the people he met, how much he earned and owed. This particular father's story cannot be told that way: he does not exist. What may exist is the man, José Bortoluci, Brazilian, son of Demétria and João, born in 1943, in the rural Campinho neighbourhood of Jaú municipality, married to Dirce, father of José Henrique and João Paulo, Catholic, truck driver, Palmeiras supporter, great cook, chronic heart patient from the age of forty-eight, retired due to disability, currently an oncological patient. That would be a biographer's task, but biographers don't examine the lives of people like him, a worker, a common man who read and wrote little, who did not run a corporation, command an army, govern a country or conquer a territory.

The way he narrates his story also seems to belie the fixation on unity and the sense of a whole life that is so central to most biographies. Sometimes I look to the thinking of Roland Barthes: against the unifying authoritarianism of the biography, I seek to draw on 'a few details, a few preferences, a few inflections, let us say: to "biographemes" whose distinction and mobility might go beyond any fate and come to touch, like Epicurean atoms, some future body'.

These Epicurean atoms travel through my father's words, uniting different times and places. They can appear in the form of a journey along the Madeira-Mamoré railroad, the notorious 'Devil's Railroad', so called because of the staggering number of workers who died during its construction at the beginning of the twentieth century:

It must have been in '67, it's been so long now I get my dates muddled. A trip came up, from São Paulo to Rio Branco do Acre, carrying machinery for a factory they were building there. But I knew there was no road from Porto Velho to Rio Branco. We had to get to Porto Velho, put our trucks on top of a train wagon and travel five hundred kilometres on the wagon. It was pure adventure, in the middle of the forest. There were six or seven little stations along the way, where the train took goods from Indians, gold prospectors, rubber tappers; the places where the train stopped were the loading points. They all had bars, with cachaça, tubaína, not much else. So, on this journey, I loaded the truck and put it on the train at Porto Velho. It didn't leave for another three days. We then spent five days travelling four hundred kilometres on that train wagon. The train had five wagons and a steam engine, powered by logs. At each stop they had to refuel the engine with wood so the combustion engine would work.

A few years later, in 1972, the 366-kilometre railroad would be deactivated. The image of an old, log-powered train slowly tearing open the forest reminds me of the delirious colonial occupation of Amazonia, the hundreds of workers who died building that railroad in the early twentieth century, the arrogant experiment of conquering the rainforest.

The old railroad is a skeletal form of Brazil's inexhaustible plans for greatness. The construction site for that diabolical railroad foreshadows those of Brasília, the Trans-Amazonian Highway, the Belo Monte dam, the stadiums built for the 2014 World Cup, and so many other projects which acted as postcards for a semblance of modernity. *Five wagons and a steam engine, powered by logs,* crossing the state of Rondônia, one of many vain, failed gestures of the 'occupation of territory' which the Brazilian brand of capitalist devastation still calls progress.

What to do with my father's words? How to hear them, transcribe them, reorganize them without losing their consistency and vibrancy?

I give up trying to name this inquiry which links together past and present, the national story and the story of a worker's life, fact and fabulation, displacements and condensations, and the spoken and the written word, different linguistic registers complicated by the act of transcription – which already involves a process of translation that is far from impartial.

By trying to reconstruct important parts of his story, the facts of his life begin to assemble on a road that opens up between me and my father. This is a story that I can only write as a son.

Questions of method and style, which took up a lot of my time at the beginning of this project, became theoretical trivialities after the medical diagnosis in December 2020. The news of cancer erupted like an emergency siren. It imposed new cables which tied us together as a family and tightened the knots between the distant past and a present that appeared to be in flames.

As we accompanied him during his hospital stays and examinations, we entered a new era, one marked by the slow time of waiting rooms and the many nights spent in hospitals, by the almost weekly journey from Jaú to São

Paulo and the care of helping him to bathe and dry himself, by the constant battle against medical bureaucracy and the recurring choice between radically different courses of treatment, by the new rhythm of changing catheters, bags and nappies. It was in this brand-new present that my ears were most receptive to my father's stories.

We did six long interviews, recording in January and February 2021. I also noted down conversations in notebooks or on my phone; I accumulated improvised, scribbled comments, sentences I'd heard over the phone, during visits to Jaú, or during the hundreds of hours we spent together in hospital and at consultations over the last two years.

In these conversations, past, present and future are in constant overlap. The person who narrates simultaneously inhabits the present tense of speaking and the time of the events being described, besides also experiencing the fraying of the edges between the two. Similarly, I – the one asking and listening – live simultaneously in the present tense of the listening, in the memories of the times in my own life when I had previously heard fragments of these stories, and in the various future tenses of listening to the recordings, reading the transcriptions and writing.

In the interviews, I try to follow the facts, ponder his word choices, carry out an excavation of his silences.

Initially, he insists he doesn't have much to say and tries to understand my motives for recording his stories. *I think you're going to keep these recordings as a memento, so you can remember my words. I hope you make the best of this time we have together, and that everything turns out right and you're happy with it.*

Sometimes we discover things that were right next to us but which we had never properly observed, like when we stare at our hands and are surprised by lines we've already seen hundreds of times. Or when we're shocked by our reflection in a mirror we didn't know was there and, for a fraction of a second, see in our own image our father's smile, our grandmother's glare, our brother's countenance, the hair of an uncle we see once a year, the posture of a great-grandfather we only know from photos.

Year after year, we're investigated by relatives and acquaintances who operate with the astuteness of a genealogist, inserting us into a centuries-old lineage of anatomy, expressions, emotions and lexica. Our bodies and our voices are constantly advertising where we came from and how to get back there – or else how to escape.

In the history of literature, few subjects have been covered more than the relationship between parents and children. It's one of the central themes in the master narratives of the West, perhaps in all cultures. None of us can escape this tragically human condition of filiation, though it does take on an immense range of forms. We are born and die alone, that's certain; but we arrive in the world surrounded by attention, by gestures and touch that mark us for the rest of our lives. Our caregivers are our connection with our contemporaries and those who preceded them. Our individual story is tethered to the current of the generations, and those who exercise the paternal and maternal functions are the boat in which we navigate the turbid river of history.

In the beginning, our parents speak through us, not just for us. They invent a voice to turn a baby's babbling into words. We then continue to be born through our own words, which we learn with our parents, without them or in opposition to them. This second birth never ends.

We spend our lives constructing our own vocabulary, composing a rhythm of speech, reinventing expressions we heard in a remote time. We use dusty words for loving and hating or for expressing fullness or hunger, just as we did at the dining table as children. To this day, I still ask for the volume of the TV to be raised, like my mother does, instead of turned up; like my grandma Isaura, I call on all the saints and the Virgin Mary when I'm surprised by something; I unexpectedly blurt out all the blasphemies I heard from my father (*Dio porco! Leper!*) and my brother and I chuckle when one of us recovers a word or expression we made up as kids.

To become an adult is to travel both nearer to and further away from that familial dialect, the vivid language of childhood. This is no easy task. We do the delayed labour of choosing some words, other words choosing us, getting rid of a lot of these words, revolting against terms and usage, building a personal archive and, with time, producing a tertiary, hesitant, interrupted narrative, like a chorus that's always out of tune, in which high notes and low notes, new words and old words, create a strange, unending dissonance.

We can only speak our own language when we settle scores with the language of our parents.

II. NOW YOU KNOW

'Everyone else's ancestors had taken part in history,
but mine seemed to have been mere lodgers in
history's house.'
— Maria Stepanova

My family's story is a small piece in the jigsaw puzzle of the
transatlantic working class – in our case, a white working
class. My grandparents and my parents are among those
workers who always received little and couldn't count
on much protection from the State, but benefitted from
what W.E.B. Du Bois called the 'public and psychological
wage' of white people – a lifelong resource we receive for
the simple fact of not being the descendants of indigenous people or enslaved Africans.

The whiteness of poor European immigrants was skilfully mobilized by the Brazilian elites in their mission to
replace the enslaved workforce in the country, promote a
politics of whitening and perpetuate a violent racial hier-
archy. And it's clear that these immigrants always enjoyed
the privileges of occupying the dominant side of that cruel
arrangement. This way of becoming part of the nation set
the tone for the private lives of these immigrants and their
experience of work in the new country: foreign men and
women, poor and illiterate upon arrival yet endowed with
that public racial benefit, a generous act of transgenera-
tional affirmative racial action, bringing them advantages
that they and their descendants could accumulate over
time.

My paternal grandfather, Joanim (no one called him
João), was the oldest son of an Italian couple. Demétria,
my paternal grandmother, was the daughter of Spaniards.

With the exception of her parents, all of my great-grand-parents were Italian, a very common occurrence in the Jaú region, which attracted a large quantity of European peasants between the final decades of the nineteenth century and the first decades of the twentieth century, most of them employed as workers on coffee plantations.

My grandpa Joanim's parents were agricultural workers from a village near Genoa. An older cousin, decades later, discovered that Giuseppe and Maria left north-eastern Italy in around 1910, headed for South America. The story of the family surname is somewhat nebulous. I recall a theory, never verified, that my great-grandfather, in Italy, was Giuseppe Bortoluzzo, but with the change of continent, language and documents, Bortoluzzo ended up becoming Bortoluzzi and then Bortolucci, with two Cs. Only my father, my brother João Paulo and I are Bortoluci, with one C – an error at the registry office amputated the second C and created this small branch of the family.

The 'new world' – Catholic, rural, patriarchal and cut through with racism and inequality – was at once similar and different to the world they had come from: poor regions of rural Italy in the late nineteenth and early twentieth centuries, the periphery of Europe's periphery. These recently arrived immigrants could nurture the dream of starting a new life, getting some money together, opening up a small business or perhaps buying a small piece of land together with brothers and cousins – as was the case with my grandpa Joanim. With that, they could aspire to have a family story that was less marked by deprivation, illiteracy and the premature death of children.

Disputes and settlements among recent immigrants from Europe to Brazil, at a time when slavery had only been abolished a few decades ago, obeyed a set of practically non-negotiable principles: marrying a poorer person, with no property and from a different European origin, was reproachable; marrying a black person inconceivable.

Demétria and Joanim were married in January 1940. My aunts, speaking in hushed voices squeezed out through their teeth, say the fact they owned a small property was sufficient reason for my grandfather's family to be suspicious of that marriage. Grandma Demétria, as well as being 'Spanish', was a landless 'settler'. Maria, my Italian great-grandmother, did not approve of the union between her son and the young washerwoman. Besides the girl's origins, there was the fact that Joanim was the oldest son and already fatherless, which would have conferred more importance upon the role his wife would occupy as a kind of second matriarch who would contest space with Nonna Maria.

It is speculated that older aunts from that side of the family had already made promises to another family, and so they wished vengeful plagues upon that union. To this day, some of my father's sisters give credence to such curses and wonder if that's why all of Grandma Demétria's daughters were widowed so young and Grandpa Joanim lost all of the little money he had.

My paternal grandparents had nine children. They were all born on the same rural property that belonged to my grandfather's family. Grandma Demétria gave birth to ten babies in ten years. Ten years pregnant, breastfeeding, carrying their weight as she worked, watching children starting and leaving school and working on the farm. She saw one of them die when others had not even come into the world. My father is the fifth, the second boy, but the oldest male to reach seven – the age at which he and his siblings began to work, helping their parents, aunts and

uncles. Not only did work became a part of life long before school did, its reach extended far beyond it, both in
hours per day and the role it played in the formation of
each boy and girl.

My father studied up to fourth grade in his rural
school in the Barra Mansa district of Jaú. *We used to play
a lot during break. Our favourite part was having snacks we
brought with us for lunch. All the kids would sit together on
the floor and share the food, we'd eat it all together, all mixed
up.* He remembers little of the classroom. He started fifth
grade, but it meant he had to take the train into the city
every day, walk several kilometres to the school and then
walk back to his family's farm, only reaching home after
three in the afternoon, which meant he couldn't work on
the farm. My father left the city school after a few months
and began working on the land full-time. He was ten.

But even this brief schooling had already conferred
some cultural distinction upon my father and his siblings
in contrast to the previous generation of my family. None
of my four grandparents attended school. As children
they all learnt to read and write at home – with the exception of my maternal grandfather, Grandpa Aristides, who
only learnt to read and write at the age of forty through
MOBRAL, the literacy programme for adults set up by
the military dictatorship as an alternative to Paulo Freire's
project. When I ask my father if my grandparents could
read and write, he replies, *Yes, they learnt alone*, taught by
uncles and aunts or older siblings who knew the basics of
letters and words.

Isaura, my maternal grandmother, had a prodigious
memory and, like my father, enjoyed telling stories.
Shortly after I first started school, when she realized I
enjoyed that world of books and classrooms, Grandma
Isaura told me she had learnt to read and write on the

36

ranch where she was born, leafing through her father's old dictionary after her eldest brother had taught her the alphabet. She used to say that for many years she dreamt of entering a classroom and sitting down at a school desk. Grandma Isaura fulfilled her dream when my mother – her oldest daughter – began her studies at the age of seven.

My father narrates the story of his life as one of work. In the social universe in which he was brought up and worked, the greatest sin is sloth, and moral vocabulary pits 'workers' against 'layabouts'. Above all, it is necessary not to be or even appear to be a layabout. Work is what gives shape to time, demarcates one life stage from the next and defines your place in the world.

Becoming a man meant distancing himself from the world of school and making manual labour the destiny of his developing body. In doing so, he could follow in his father's footsteps.

I started working on a tractor at the age of seven, ploughing earth. At the time, Grandpa Joanim had a small plot with his brothers, and they had a little tractor. And you know what kids are like... I'd watch Grandpa driving, then get up into the tractor. In the old days, tractors were exactly like the toys you have today, real small, but I was even smaller. Since there was no way I could work sitting on the seat, I'd ride standing on the step. Ploughing earth all day long. I'd finish school, go to the farm, stay until five or six in the evening. That was my life from seven to ten, which was when I left school and just worked. At fifteen, my parents moved to the city, and I started working in a garage. I worked in that garage for seven years. It was like this: from seven to fourteen I worked with the tractor, from fourteen to around twenty-one I worked as a mechanic, and at twenty-two I left the mechanic trade and went on the road.

37

The families of two of my grandfather's brothers also lived on the farm. Sixteen children who grew up together, living between school and the house, between play and work.

Our job was to gather calves in the evening, milk cows in the morning, peel the corn to give to the pigs, attend to the hens... The oldest girls were still looking after the youngest. Playing at trucks, milking, gathering fruit; that was what we played at.

The games were a way of preparing yourself for a life of work. My aunts played at cooking and sewing. My mother, a seamstress almost her whole life, learnt her trade as a child making clothes for Pelada, her hen who had been born without any feathers.

Of the seven of my father's siblings who reached adolescence, only the youngest two continued their studies beyond the fifth grade. One of them, Paulo, trained as a turner on a technical course and moved at a young age to São Bernardo, where he was employed for his entire life in metal factories until, at sixty, just a few months before retirement, he suffered a fatal heart attack. The youngest studied medicine, with the help of his siblings. *We managed to put Toninho, who was the baby, through medical school; but his career too ended in the blink of an eye, he also died at sixty-odd.*

I was struck by his use of the verb *formar* – to graduate, but also to shape or form – when talking about putting his younger brother through medical school: the idea of being able to 'form' or 'shape' someone as a group, as a shared mission; and especially to collectively form a younger brother, which was fairly typical in working-class families of that generation.

The sisters: three seamstresses and a younger aunt who

worked her whole life – she's still working, at seventy-three – in a wide variety of positions in different shops and schools. And Uncle Nelson, a year younger than my father, also a truck driver, who died around the age of fifty-eight from complications following a stroke. *He died on the day of the 2002 World Cup final, when Brazil became champions for the fifth time. I didn't even watch the game.*

His brother Roberto, a year older than him, died at five, the way poor children living in rural areas often used to: sudden stomach pain, precarious medical care, premature death.

What did he die of? Ah, I don't know, he just died. He died shortly after he got to the city doctor... No one can convince me it wasn't a damn appendicitis. He had this terrible pain, everyone on the farm was making him tea and praying, and when they saw he was getting worse, the fever was ramping up, they took him to Jaú. He was probably dead on arrival.

Because he was the oldest male child to reach adolescence, my father took on the role of my grandfather's principal assistant.

He tells me that his father had to *become a man* very early on and help his mother look after his siblings. *Grandpa Joanim was the head of the family, he was the head of all his brothers and sisters.* At a young age he started to take on greater and greater responsibilities on the farm where they lived, since his father had died when he was still a teenager. Like my father, my grandfather also grew up with seven siblings. And like him, he was known for being able to build or fix anything.

And he liked hunting. My father loved to accompany him, walking behind Grandpa Joanim, running after the quails or partridges he shot. When his most beloved hunting dog became sick, it fell to my father to sacrifice him.

He was an incredibly able setter, Molerão. Killing him was too painful for my grandfather.

There was nothing to be done. The dog had a tumour in its head this big, it was in loads of pain. Your grandpa said to me: 'Put him to sleep; grab the shotgun and go up to the top of the hill; once you're up there, shoot him in the head and come back.' So, me and the dog head out of the house and up to an out-of-the-way spot on top of a hill. Even with his sickness, you should have seen how happy he was: Molerão's looking at me holding the shotgun, thinking we're going hunting. He runs ahead, comes back, sniffs at me. And then the moment came when I had to shoot him.

My father was twelve, and I must have been the same age when I heard the story for the first time. At twelve, he had already left school and was carrying out such missions. I think about my adolescent father, carrying out a sacrifice on his father's behalf, to spare him the pain. One more boy in a line of sons who, when called up by their fathers – or forced to grow up prematurely because of a father's absence – have no option other than to answer, 'Here I am.' To become a man was to learn to work like your father and to look after the family, but also to use violence when necessary, to be prepared to take your father's gun and carry out a bloody act of compassion.

When I went up there to kill Molerão, I took Grandpa Joanim's double-barrelled shotgun. He told me: 'Get up real close and shoot him in the head, so you don't miss.' The shots from that gun were big, round slugs, there was no way you could miss. As I listen, I think the opposite; there were lots of ways you could have missed. But I say nothing.

My grandfather Joanim took my father with him to Paraná when he invested all the money he had, the savings from decades of work, in a small coffee plantation. My father tells how my grandfather's brothers divided up the farm in Jaú and, with his share, Grandpa Joanim bought some land in northern Paraná. They went there in my grandfather's old Chevrolet; the journey along mud tracks took a whole day.

Down there, in Paraná, there was nothing but coffee. There were coffee plants that looked like mango trees, it was wild. The plantation was almost finished, the first harvest was about to happen. That soil was so fertile it was scary, and the coffee came out almost black. Only there was a big frost.

My father, at fourteen or fifteen, helped my grandfather put up the fence, build the storehouse and prepare the land on the farm the family planned to move to. They were there for a month, a month and a half, working together.

What happened next is why your grandpa died with nothing. He'd bought the farm with the portion of the money he'd got from selling his part of the other one; he spent all that money on the land in Paraná and borrowed a little more, which he was going to pay off with the coffee harvest that was on the way; but then the frost came, and he lost everything. Everything. He had to go to the bank, remortgage the whole plot. And just when the coffee was about to be harvested again, another frost. He burnt it down to the stumps again, for a second time, right down to the ground. Such a bad frost he had to burn it all, what an ugly thing. So, my father does what he has to do: sells the land to pay off the bank and we go back home with nothing.

The first time he told me this story, when I was around twenty, he concluded the narrative with this verdict: *now you know your story.* To know my story was to discover how the class destiny which defined the social place in which I was born and raised was perpetuated. The coffee plants ready to harvest on the small property in Paraná were the wager made by my grandfather and my young father, a chance to live a more prosperous, secure life, to start a trajectory less marked by the spectre of unpaid bills, debt collection, exhausting and alienating work in exchange for risible salaries. A dream of improving your life – only there was a big frost.

The day his mother died, in 2008, when for a brief moment it was just the two of us sitting by her body, I heard my father quietly lamenting: *She's leaving nothing behind.* I imagine he wasn't so much speaking as a son sorry that he wasn't receiving a part of some material inheritance, but more as a father fearful of also 'leaving nothing behind', of ending up one day as another turn of the cycle of the reproduction of the working class in a country noted for its inequality, our cruel collective condition. At that moment, he was not only talking to his dead mother but to me and my brother, to our future selves who would one day keep vigil over the inert body of our father. Those two maxims – *and now you know your story*; *leaving nothing behind* – were his way of telling the story of the failure of a project of social ascent that connected two continents and four generations of his family.

In January 2015, the night before another risky heart operation, he calculated out loud how much his boss owed him – two or three accrued holidays, one late salary payment, a bit of cash to be reimbursed. It wasn't much, but not much is more than nothing. It was just the two of us, alone in a stuffy hospital room. He was making an oral inventory of his assets, a gesture which condensed into a modest figure his history of work, and which he addressed to me like a brief, improvised will.

Just as one is not born, but rather becomes, a woman, one

also becomes a man in a specific historical context, within certain social relations and under the watchful eye of certain cultural values and codes. In my father's case, the universe in which he forged his masculinity was that of traditional, hierarchical family relationships, imbibed in a moralistic, Catholic language typical of rural São Paulo state in the mid-twentieth century, and a professional category in which rigid patriarchal codes operated.

To this day, my father understands that his worth as a man is linked to his work, to his role as a provider, to his ability to resolve everyday problems. He has authoritarian outbursts when things don't go according to his expectations – even the smallest things, like when we don't immediately sit down at the table for lunch when he calls us. He snorts every time someone interrupts him speaking. The tone of his voice oscillates between jovial enthusiasm and annoyed peevishness. He always complains at the television, he argues back at it, it enrages him.

He never thought my mother needed to learn to drive, and he made it hard for her to work as a seamstress, maid or any of the other occupations she has had in her life. For him, the world is divided into men's things and women's things – except for cooking, which confounds that traditional division, since in my parents' house the kitchen is his space too.

He spent his early adulthood in the urban part of Jaú, where he moved with his family at fifteen, after the failure of the Paraná project. To be young and a man there meant a life of toil, but also one of boozing and partying. The daily ritual of drinking cachaça with colleagues, cousins or local friends was sacred.

And the frequent trips to brothels. Traditional Brazilian Catholicism never railed against men's right to pay for sex; it always considered prostitutes to be modern incarnations of witches, and prostitution as a necessary evil for the preservation of the patriarchal order which rested on the inalienable sexual rights of men and the sexual subjugation of women.

Several of the old, grand houses near the bus station in Jaú were brothels, always open, two blocks away from the Municipal Chamber and the parish church. Church, brothel and chamber formed a sort of political holy trinity in the country's interior: Catholicism, patriarchal masculinity and local political factionism.

My father was an attractive young man. In the 3 x 4" photo of him aged eighteen, wearing his military service uniform, his hair is short and spiky. Normally he wore it longer, combed back. He always had a lot of hair – still does. His light eyes stand out in his thin face, a thinness he would lose over the coming years, especially from twenty-two onwards, when he began driving a truck. During his compulsory military service, he was known for escaping the barracks to attend bars and parties in the city's clubs. On one of these escapades, he was caught at a dance by his commander, who punished him by making him clean the barracks for several weeks. On another adventure, he signed up for a ten-kilometre race in the city but abandoned it after a few metres and appeared washed, combed and in his Sunday best to greet his mother and sisters, eagerly awaiting him at the finishing line.

His stories from this era are characterized by repeated scenes: the skill with which he repaired engines, the binges that hospitalized him on several occasions, the big parties at my grandparents' house with a large crowd of brothers and their girlfriends, nephews, aunts, uncles.

I imagine he must also have been seductive, or cocky at least. He never had girlfriends before my mother, which doesn't mean he didn't have lots of sexual flings and affairs. 'Ever stayed there, Dad?' I ask jokingly, pointing to the small jail near Jaú's main police station. *Yes, but only for one night.* I'm surprised, and he is too, to find that it turned out to be a legitimate question. But once the event has been revealed, he tells me he spent a night locked up there as a youth after being apprehended by police in the outskirts of Jaú, screwing a girl in the middle of a cane field in his father's old DKW, which he drove when he was in the town for this purpose, among others.

My father was never interested in politics. For him, as for many of his friends and acquaintances, politics appears as a seasonal phenomenon, mainly during elections, even then inciting no passion whatsoever. His theory is that it doesn't matter which candidate wins in the elections, because *whatever happens, we still have to get up and go to work the next day.*

What is apparent in this idea, once again, is his ethical cartography, which divides the world between righteous people and layabouts (whether they're rich or poor, political or not). In this worldview, politics is full of layabouts; the 'righteous' politicians are the exception, and their integrity has little to do with their ideology or party ties. The two most important questions are: Is this politician a decent person? Has my life improved or got worse in recent years? These two questions structure a way of visualizing the State and politics that, for him, is more concrete than the ideas mobilized by intellectual elites to give meaning to the terrain of politics (democracy, fascism, socialism, left, right...).

My grandfather Joanim, on the other hand, seems to have been a far more interested observer of the political stage in Brazil and in the Italy of his parents. He listened

45

to *A Voz do Brasil* every night and a painting of Mussolini hung for many years on the wall of the rural house where my father and his brothers grew up. For Joanim's children, Mussolini was 'the old man on the wall'.

The painting was in the living room. He loved that old man there on the wall. But then, when me and him were in Paraná, building a storehouse for the coffee, my family moved from the farm to the city. We were there for thirty or forty days, I think. During that time, my mother and siblings came to Jaú; they decided to move to the city because there was nothing left at the farm... They rented a house here. They came, and during the move they got rid of the painting. My mother didn't want to bring that old man hanging on the wall – she threw it away. And my father was really upset when he arrived and couldn't see the painting of the old man. He kept shouting, 'Where's Mussolini? Where's Mussolini?'

I only heard this story a few years ago. Many children of Italians during this period felt an affection for the Fascist leader and did not forgive Vargas's pact with the Allies in the Second World War, after years spent flirting with the Axis. I don't know if that was the case with my grandfather, and I never will. I don't know what he thought about Mussolini and fascism, or why that old man on the wall meant so much to him.

I asked my father what he knew about Mussolini. *Some Italian guy. Don't ask me about all that political crap.*

When I was seven, my father returned to Jaú with severe chest pains. At the time, he was working in Vargem Grande do Sul, a city in the north of São Paulo state. His condition was very serious. I remember visiting him in Jaú's St Judas Hospital, around New Year's Day in 1993, before his departure for Ribeirão Preto, where he was to undergo a delicate heart operation. My brother, my mother and I walked up those springy ramps to find him. The hospital had yellowed walls, a palette of tired and humid colours which only old hospitals can produce with the slow accumulation of all kinds of humours. And then a small, very white room where my father, frail, dressed in blue robes, was taken by a nurse. I knew it could be the final goodbye.

He survived the surgery with immense scars, four bypasses, a mammary bypass, a daily arsenal of medications and a routine of consultations and periodical examinations that would be with him forever. From that point on, I found, for many years, that I had to keep watch over his life – a solidifying of what I had felt since my early childhood, when I would throw away lighters and cigarette packets when he wasn't watching. It scared me when he overate, and he never gave up his big portions of meat, seasoning everything with lots of oil and salt and drinking on the weekends. Seeing him drink beer at family celebrations made me feel deeply sad and terrifyingly powerless. I wasn't alone: I was echoing and amplifying my mother's fear. When the doctor who first operated on his heart found out he had been smoking for decades (three packs of Hollywood a day, one cigarette almost lighting the next), he suggested she give him cigarettes if she wanted to be a widow.

My father went back to driving his truck one year after the surgery. From then on, he lived in Jaú and was employed by a transporter of sand and stone. For the next twenty years he worked from Monday to Saturday, from four in the morning to six in the evening.

With this new job, after a year of abstinence, he began coming home stinking of cigarettes. My mother could smell my father's hands and clothes and I could too, from afar and from close up, mixed in with the scent of sweat and dust that he carried after a day's work. He was always one step ahead of all our questions, telling us all his colleagues smoked.

Almost two years without smoking. Then I started at that sand-hauling firm and on the first trip I bought a filthy pack of smokes. I came home stinking. 'I was near so and so, he smokes' – that's what I told you, your mother and João. Until one day, when you caught me smoking. It was the last cigarette I ever put in my mouth. Do you remember? It was during the parade for the anniversary of Jaú. João was marching. I went to park the car and came back smoking, I thought you'd be further away by then. We got home and you wouldn't stop crying on the sofa, do you remember? And I said: I've already thrown the cigarettes away, and may the devil save the worst place in hell for me if I ever put another one in my mouth again. I never smoked again and I never will. But sometimes I still think about those damn cigarettes...

In recent months I have thought countless times about Telemachus, son of Ulysses, and the anonymous son in 'The Third Bank of the River', Guimarães Rosa's astonishing short story. Both sons of travellers, of different kinds of men who are always leaving and whose return is uncertain. There's a kinship between them, despite the huge distance and the many centuries separating ancient Ithaca and the backlands of Minas Gerais, on the fringes of modernity. Both are in search of fathers who are present and absent, who at times send subtle, ambiguous signals, who inhabit a liminal space between life and death, between the noise of the human masses and the mysterious immensity of the waters.

Telemachus launches himself into the sea in search of a father he cannot see, but whose stories he picks up along the way. The anonymous son by the riverbank awaits the return of a father he can see but who says nothing. These fathers present an almost indecipherable enigma, and both sons experience the desire and the fear that the father will return.

In 'The Third Bank of the River', after the long-awaited wave from the father, the son confesses: 'I experienced the dreadful sense of cold that comes from deadly fear, and I became ill.'

Is it in fact possible to return home after doing battle, seeing magical beings, confronting profound solitude, experiencing the world?

When I was five, my father brought me a little plastic horse during one of his transits through our house. Before he left, I placed the hidden toy in his suitcase so he wouldn't forget me.

At seven, I asked my parents to take me to the Jaú municipal library. We had no books at home save the Bible, a few catechisms and some prayer books. That same year, I asked for a globe as a present. I was interested in the world and was already thinking of it using representations and vocabularies that differed from those I had heard from my parents.

Around the same time, I started playing Jesus Christ on stage during Sunday Mass, at the Santa Casa chapel in Jaú, where my brother and I sang in the infant chorus and were later altar boys. For years I repeated the words of the Gospels, staged the multiplication of the loaves and the healing of the sick, while learning to raise the pitch of my voice. This altar voice still inhabits my speech.

From the moment I started school I was treated by teachers, headteachers and classmates as a little academic prodigy. These recognitions took the form of immaculate school reports, essay competition prizes, trips to international congresses and meetings, presidency of the student council and of state-wide student parliaments, articles in the school and city newspapers, study grants, my name at the top of competitions and entrance exams and, beyond school, first-class honours degrees.

In a recurring childhood dream, I would lead my friends to our school library to save them from an enormous monster attacking the city. We would be safe in the library.

Barthes, also a traveller between languages, notes that 'the subject's native language ages – all the more because it's always the language of the class origins of the parents – at a rate that's difficult to measure because the changes occur daily'. At thirteen I had almost completely lost my Jaú accent, with its Rs typical of the caipira dialect and its cutting Ts and Ds. Language is another kind of home, and by changing mine I was signalling the direction my own life would take. Consciously or otherwise, I was trying to open paths to another way of inhabiting the world while I still lived in my childhood home.

The biographical gulf separating me from my parents widened with each school year, with each medal in a Maths or Astronomy Olympiad and each interview with a regional newspaper or TV channel, eagerly reporting the academic feats of that small-town boy, the son of workers, public school pupil and then scholarship student.

Even without fully understanding what each one of those conquests meant, my parents always celebrated them more than I did. They narrated these achievements to anyone who would listen, in queues for the bakery, waiting rooms or chats after Mass. My mother kept every one of the reports, medals and diplomas in a blue folder; my brother had to live with the constant comparisons

('Which one of you is more intelligent?'); my father sold raffle tickets and asked for money from friends to help with some of my trips.

I took a long time to understand that my success at school was not just my own but the result of a family undertaking.

III. URGE TO SEE

'The swallows are back
And I'm back too.'
—— Trio Parada Dura, 'As andorinhas' ['The Swallows']

Between the ages of fifteen and twenty-two, my father worked in a garage for heavy-duty vehicles. Grandpa Joanim took my father to Mr Ítalo's garage and asked if the Italian mechanic had a job for his oldest son. Mr Ítalo was a short, stubborn man with strong arms and a red face, whose breath stank of cachaça and chewing tobacco. He taught my father to fix engines, weld car bodywork, resolve mechanical problems, build metal frames. Until a few years ago, the gate to the land where the garage once stood was the same one my father built and installed when he worked there, something he never stopped mentioning whenever we walked past.

My father was surrounded by men much older than him, his colleagues or the clients who brought their tractors and trucks to be repaired at the garage. *There were mechanics there who'd been working for ten, fifteen years and had never built an engine. I'd started building them within two years of working there. I was in love with engines.*

That was also where he began to live out his own Bildungsroman as a young man in a small inland town during the 1950s. As well as working, he drank and smoked with his older colleagues in Dona Iolanda's bar, right opposite the workshop. That was where he fell into an alcoholic coma that became a family legend: at sixteen, after fixing a huge German engine from a ceramics factory, a task many of his colleagues had thought impossible, he went on a bender that left him unconscious in hospital for three days. My grandma Demétria cried

53

by his bedside, certain she was about to lose another child.

Mr Ítalo's garage was also a place for hearing and telling stories. The old man with the heavy accent liked to share memories from his boyhood: the devil appearing on a river shore, the sounds of bombs and gunfire during times of war, legends from country life in southern Italy.

My father heard many tales from truck drivers there. Anonymous workers, many of them from outside the city, who were passing through Jaú and needed to get their vehicles checked before returning to the tarmac. It was them, and their stories, that awoke him to other worlds, other desires.

I was a good mechanic, I learnt fast, liked fixing engines. But when a truck showed up at the garage the drivers began to tell us about their travels. I was hooked, I wanted to know what it was like. I had an urge to see these places, to know them, to discover the hardships they told us about, experience the adventures for myself. So I became an adventurer.

Being a truck driver at that time meant clinging to the hope of economic progression as an autonomous professional. The work offered the promise that a young man (there were almost no women in the business) could became a kind of small-scale entrepreneur, without needing a diploma or financial support from well-off parents or the State.

Between 1960 and 1980, few drivers were employed by carrier companies. Most in the profession drove their own trucks, generally portioned into dozens of loan payments that were rarely paid off early. That was the case with my father, a self-employed driver for thirty years, always concerned with paying off his loans. Trucks aged rapidly on the precarious highways of the time; drivers had to exchange them for newer vehicles or invest in costly replacement parts so that they could traverse the country's huge distances on roads with no tarmac, covered in mudholes, expanses of virgin forest, stretches of road still under construction, and other obstacles.

Getting credit was easy, and the international brands kept releasing new models. The country's industrial estate was expanding and the demand for new truck models was growing, especially during the years of the so-called 'economic miracle' between the end of the 1960s and the mid-1970s. This illusory 'miracle' was conditional upon the existence of trucks in a continental country that had almost no railways and a meagre waterway network for transporting cargo.

I was always coming and going. It went like this: I'd load up in São Paulo and go to Boa Vista, unload there and load for Belém, load in Belém and go to São Luís de Maranhão, load in São Luís and go to Recife... We'd stop and get the next load. I'd keep doing that all the way back to São Paulo and then return home. Every time I left Jaú, I didn't know when I'd be back.

'Progress' was the military government's watchword, measured in kilometres of new roads, new factories, airports. Progress was our enormous white whale, forever in flight, and the trucks were ships loaded with men looking for sustenance, fortune and adventure, men who were the arms and the wheels in service of the grandiloquent plans of generals and businessmen locked away in distant cabinets, offices, barracks and basements.

The truck was not only an instrument of work, but an investment which demanded years of effort and big loans. With arduous work, often driving through the night under the influence of chemical stimulants, the driver hoped to pay off the loan he took out to buy his truck and improve his family's financial condition – buy some land to build a house on, put more food on the table, buy new furniture from the department stores opening all over the country, go to the beach once a year. With luck, perhaps, he could one day exchange his truck for a newer or better one, or even start the payments on a second vehicle, with dreams of owning a small fleet, becoming an entrepreneur, hiring other drivers to drive their trucks.

This script rarely plays out. *Of all my truck driver pals, only one got rich: Braga. He managed to set up a transportation company. He delivered stone and sand all over this region. He had eight or nine trucks. But his heart did for him, he wasn't even fifty. His kids managed to fritter away everything he built. There's no more transportation, no more trucks, no more nothing.*

The tenets of entrepreneurship are nothing new among the Brazilian working classes. The dream of being your own boss always went hand in hand with the dream of owning your own home, and both represented risks for workers: the spectre of debt, the scourge of interest, the very real possibility of losing everything and having nowhere to turn. As a self-employed driver, my father paid national insurance for years so that he could retire with the most basic state pension, after decades of exhausting work.

To earn the full freight, truck drivers had to deliver the cargo by the agreed date. They received ten or fifteen per cent of the freight on departure – enough money, at a push, to cover the costs of the outward journey. The rest was paid upon delivery, and there was always the risk that the person receiving the cargo would have the nerve to try to haggle over the amount initially agreed, because of delays, avarice or for completely arbitrary reasons. My father tells me that the final freight for long journeys always felt like a decent amount of real money, but that initial sensation rapidly dissolved: the maintenance costs were never-ending, there was always some part that needed changing, the petrol ate into your wallet and the loan payments never stopped. In the end, there was never much money to take home.

Who were these men of the road? Despite the importance of truckers to the country's economic life during the dictatorship, representations of the aspirations and disappointments of an existence behind the wheel by Brazil's arts and culture industry have been scarce. There have been very few truck driver characters in TV soaps, films or books, and these workers never occupied a key position in the various imaginings of the country formulated during that period by different artistic or political movements.

Of course, this lack of representation is not confined to truck drivers, but is symptomatic of the enormous limitations of Brazil's cultural elites when it comes to creating images of the people that are in dialogue with workers' real lives, with their cultural universes, their aesthetics and their diverse political grammars. In the art of that period, 'the people' generally appear as an abstract category, or in the repeated formula of a 'pre-revolutionary people' in the mould of the Marxism of the time; or else as manifestations of a 'folkloric people', rural, romantic and pre-modern. In most cases, real workers, in their immense diversity, hardly correspond to these models at all.

It fell to popular genres to develop some of the most meaningful representations of the lives of truck drivers.

Jorge, um Brasileiro [Jorge, a Brazilian], a 1967 book by Oswaldo França Júnior, found some success among the public, later serving as the basis for the eponymous film directed by Paulo Thiago in 1988. In language somewhat reminiscent of the soap opera, both book and film portray a long-distance truck driver confronting his employers' avarice and the difficulties of everyday life on the roads.

More popular was the series *Carga Pesada* [Heavy Load], shown by the Globo network in 1979 and then refilmed and aired between 2003 and 2007. Both the original version and the remake narrated the adventures, romances and challenges of the charismatic trucker duo Pedro and Bino, played by Antônio Fagundes and Stênio Garcia. Pedro embodies the archetype of the truck driver as free man – fearless, seeking women and adventures – while Bino is his realist antithesis, a family man with his feet firmly on the ground, concerned with his accounts and with the future.

Probably, however, sertanejo music is the genre that has contributed most to the formation of images and narratives about the lives of professional truck drivers. Milionário and José Rico, one of the genre's most important duos, recorded 'Estrada da vida' ['Road of Life'] in 1977, a song that became the pair's biggest hit and one of the most frequently played on radio programmes dedicated to sertanejo, like the ones that formed the background music to my childhood. The two singers encapsulate the popular style of Brazil's interior, of the man who has 'succeeded in life' and likes to show off his economic success, ornamented with gold chains, cowboy hats, leather jackets, aviator shades and a huge gold-buckled belt.

The duo's artistic name and their performance heralded a promise of prosperity for those with the courage to take on the enormous obstacles of work, life, music and the highways. The song was also used as a device for the 1980 film *Na estrada da vida* [On the Road of Life]. Starring the two singers and directed by Nelson Pereira dos Santos, the sertanejo musical documentary and road movie recorded the singers on their travels around Brazil.

And yet, the sad tone of 'Estrada da vida' seems to contradict this aesthetic of prosperity. The long road of promises, of incessant running in the quest to achieve 'first place', culminates with a fatally sad conclusion – and the illusions of progress are undone.

> On this long road of life
> I'm running and I can't stop
> Hoping to be the champion
> Come in first place...
>
> But time closed in on me
> And tiredness overcame me
> My vision has darkened
> And the end of the race has come.

It's time that is closing in on the narrator of this song; time that catches up with everyone. It presents a tragic vision of the odyssey of the working class, but above all of the truck driver, through whom the drama plays out in its most literal sense.

In the song 'Sonho de um caminhoneiro' ['A Truck Driver's Dream'], also by Milionário and José Rico, two friends act out the fantasies of a legion of drivers.

> They were two inseparable friends
> Fighting for life and bread
> Carrying a dream from city to city
> Of owning their trucks

59

> With lots of struggle and sacrifice
> To pay off the loans on time
> Their dream finally came true
> The worker is now the boss.

Tragedy also rears its head in this song, not through the slow decline of time but by interrupting suddenly and catastrophically in the form of an accident which cuts short the life of one of the truck drivers:

> But cruel and treacherous fate
> Marked the time and place
> The light rain and the wet road
> They crashed into a trailer.

The other driver dies when the loan payments for the truck he bought are almost finished and his wife is pregnant with their first child.

Between the sixties and the nineties, I worked all over Brazil, I can't even remember all the sites. I took materials to Manaus International Airport... I worked there for a while. There was no road back then. To get to Manaus you had to put your truck on a watercraft and travel down the river for five days. I also worked in Guarulhos International Airport. I hauled a lot of building materials on the road from Mogi das Cruzes to Bertioga when they were opening it up, laying tarmac. I worked on the Imigrantes highway and the Bandeirantes too.

I took a lot of cargo up to Angra dos Reis when they were making the nuclear plant. I helped to open up the Trans-Amazonian Highway: I'd take a consignment, spend three weeks, a month doing something and then come back. I helped to do the asphalt on the Belém-Brasília highway, worked there for five years when it was still a dirt road. I worked at the Tucuruí plant in Pará too, as well as taking goods to Itaipu. Over in the Serra Pelada, in the seventies, eighties, the truck drivers took equipment and materials so that they could break up the earth to extract the gold: tractor parts, tools for perforating the earth, mercury, bombs for getting rid of water.

I worked in all the good places and in some bad places too.

In the late 1960s and early 1970s, Brazil's annual growth was eight per cent and the outskirts of the cities expanded with favelas and self-built neighbourhoods, some of them dotted with social housing projects. Economic growth was built on the backs of workers, who laboured to pay off vehicle loans, buy cement and bricks so they could finally build their children's bedrooms or finish paying for a piece of land in these neighbourhoods that were developing rapidly because of their work. That urban proletariat class, underpaid and in frenetic expansion since the 1940s, had to dedicate their weekends and holidays to building their own houses and those of their friends and relatives, often as a joint effort and without the support of qualified professionals or government power.

For the first time, attractive, mass-produced consumer items populated the worlds of the working classes, a universe made of sugar and colouring, plastic and transistors, metal and petrol. Colourful promises arrived through Globo TV dramas, and in the pages of weekly magazines and photo comics, in fantasies of fast cars and the saccharine romances depicted by crooners on the *Jovem Guarda* TV show. Dreams of becoming middle class, helped by the rhetoric of the 'economic miracle', were disseminated during those decades when official policy generated a dizzying rise in the concentration of revenue, national debt and urban inequality.

61

Money has a different life in each of the social worlds in which it circulates. Among working-class people there is much less embarrassment attached to discussions of how much you earn and spend, how much rent you pay, the cost of a car or how much a relative owes a moneylender. An individual can have their value recognized according to various metrics, certainly, but one of the most formidable is being seen as someone who has 'succeeded in life' thanks to hard work, and not through trickery or theft. The fundamental law – 'don't be a layabout' – operates as a guiding principle for assessing the wealth or woe of others as well as oneself.

For years my father asked me how much I earned, how much rent I paid, how much I'd spent on a trip, buying books or a new mobile phone. I was always hesitant to respond. I was proud of keeping this part of my life private, conducting it far from his and my mother's eyes. My approach to my finances is radically different from the way they treat theirs: in my parents' house, money is not an abstraction but a very present, physical object which passes from hand to hand, since they never use debit or credit cards and the little left over from their pensions has always been kept in a metal tin in the kitchen cupboard, within reach of any of us, should we need to buy a few small things.

It was only when I began writing this book that I told him how much I earned. I don't know why exactly. Perhaps because only then had I understood that knowing someone's salary had a very different meaning for me and for my parents. *I'm not asking you for my own sake, it's just pride.*

The word 'mudhole' appears with terrifying frequency

in my father's stories. Mudholes characterize his memory of the roads more than any other element of the landscape.

Most of the roads were dirt tracks, dust clouds, pools of mud. During rainy seasons, the mudholes were so bad that sometimes you were stuck for five, six, seven days without being able to move your truck. We'd drive in groups of five or six trucks, and when one sank and couldn't get out, we had to tie up two or three trucks to get it out. I'll never forget those experiences, whereas I hardly remember any of the beautiful places I've been, because you just drive through them, admire the scenery for a moment and then you're gone. Whereas a mudhole, as ugly as it is, you're stuck there for a week, see? I'd play some tapes, chat to the guys to pass the time. Sometimes there'd be a roadside stall nearby and we'd sit there and have a few drinks. So that's what I remember; it stays in your head, you never forget it.

A pragmatic spirit and a certain inclination towards minimalism were of fundamental importance in confronting the challenges of the road. To this day, my father dislikes decoration, adornment, excess. *Fussiness.* For him, things must be just what they are, without adding too many features beyond what defines them.

Back then, we used to just go around in shorts, bare-chested and with a cap on our heads. That was my worker's uniform. Sandals on my feet, barefoot sometimes if I had to walk on mud. We had to get used to the sun. Our skin became crusty, thick. Now I'm old, my skin is like paper, any kind of knock and it starts bleeding.

I think about this system of ordering and attitude towards one's own body as a pragmatic aesthetic which he still follows: plants occupy too much space inside the house, ornaments on top of cupboards gather dust,

complicated ingredients are no better than garlic and on-
ion, clothes just make you hot – so he goes bare-chested
when it's warm and doesn't care if he's sitting down to eat or
receiving guests.

Many truck drivers treat the road as a home, or as an
extension of their bodies. It was no different with my
father, but his choice of equipment and the way he dec-
orated his vehicles were always austere. *In those days, I
always had a small fan in the cab, a tape player and radio,
some tapes of sertanejo, Raul Seixas, Roberto Carlos, Secos &
Molhados, Nelson Gonçalves. Because the radio almost never
worked out there in the sticks... I wasn't really the type to have
words written on my truck. The only thing I did have on my
bumper was this: 'My qualities make up for my defects'. It
was a line from a song from the time, Roberto Carlos, I think.
Jaques, that joker, when he saw it, he asked me: 'What qualities
are those, Didi?'*

When I was in Russia for an Astronomy Student
Olympiad in 2002, I took a bus to one of the observato-
ries we were visiting, a radio telescope built in the 1960s.
It was a mysteriously immense piece of equipment. For
some time, it was one of the most modern in the world,
and several discoveries about the universe's background
radiation and the composition of stars were made there.
In radio telescopes like this one, radiation from space is
reflected by panels that form a vast circle, like an oval sta-
dium made of plaques whose inclination can be adjusted.
The rays are then captured by a receiver located in a vehicle which is positioned according to the part of the sky you
want to observe and the inclination of the panels. To mark
where the carts should be stationed, Russian scientists used
old yellow measuring tapes stretched out on the ground
– simple, cheap objects, the kind my mother has at home

and which can be found in any old cupboard. But they work well enough for that purpose, despite not looking good in photos and imbuing the space – which otherwise looks like something out of an Andrei Tarkovsky film – with a sense of improvisation and precarity.

Soon after, when I was back on board the Soviet-era bus, I saw that the hot air vents were made of cut-up pieces of PVC piping. Just like the measuring tape on the ground by the radio telescope, they did what was expected of them. I immediately thought of my father, who would definitely have solved such problems with this same disdain for aesthetics I had been so stunned by. And I believe that, had he had the opportunity to study, he would have become an engineer in the Soviet style.

He likes deep plates and uses his knife to spread the teeth of his fork apart: it's easier to pick up the food that way, with the fork splayed out like an open hand.

All truck drivers must have an inclination towards aesthetic functionalism. A truck driver must be a problem solver – which doesn't mean he doesn't appreciate beautiful things – but he knows that what matters most is that things work, and if they work there's no need to decorate them or add unnecessary layers. Perhaps becoming middle class means learning to add layers.

It was the late seventies. Rainy season, mid-December. I unloaded a cargo of brazilwood in Porto Alegre that I'd brought from Belém, and the guy was like: 'Jaú, I have a shipment of wine for Boa Vista.' 'When for?' 'Christmas.' 'Not enough time,' I said, 'it's five days until Christmas, and it's nine, ten days from here, more with all these mudholes.'

I was determined to just unload in Porto Alegre and spend Christmas at home. He went on and on and on at me... And then he said, 'While you make your mind up, I'll start loading

*your truck.' That made me angry. 'What needs to be delivered?'
'Twenty-five-litre flagons of wine. The whole load's only six
thousand kilos,' he said. My truck was new that year, this was
in '77. I'd put in a new suspension system so it would stay soft,
there was nothing but holes up north.*

*The guy says, 'You going or not?' And I say, 'Yeah, but I
won't get there till after Christmas.' 'They're completely out
of wine in Roraima,' he says, 'if you get there after Christmas
the freight is this much, but if you can get there on Christmas
Eve, I'll give you this much more. And if only ten flagons or less
break along the way, you'll get even more.'*

*He loaded up the wine. I left that afternoon, crossed the state
of Rio Grande do Sul, then the state of Santa Catarina. It was
four in the morning, almost dawn, when I arrived in the state
of Paraná. I pulled over at a petrol station, slept, and woke up
at eight-thirty. I knew I wouldn't get there, there was no way
I'd get there.*

*So far it had been tarmac roads, it was easy. I crossed
Paraná, entered the state of São Paulo, had lunch not far from
here, near Sorocaba. I ate in twenty minutes, got back in the
truck and bam! Then I started getting carried away, and I really believed I could do it: if I get to Cuiabá by early evening,
I think I've got a chance of getting to Boa Vista by Christmas.*

*The road plays tricks on us. Sometimes it seems like when
you need it, everything goes wrong but sometimes everything
can go right too.*

*I ate, stocked up on supplies, there was no one else around.
Later, I grabbed a sandwich and ate it while driving.
Everything was going right. I stopped for a shower and some
food and thought: I'll sleep in Jangada, a little place sixty kilometres past Cuiabá. There was a dirt track there. If I leave at
the crack of dawn, there's a chance I'll reach Boa Vista.*

*I got to Jangada, slept, and the next day I left early, got go-
ing, almost reached Porto Velho. All earth, mud, holes, puddles.*

From Amazonas onwards, the main danger was mudholes. I almost got to Porto Velho, slept, early the next day I crossed on the ferry to Manaus. From there it was eight hundred kilometres on a road with a tiny amount of tarmac, this wide; you had to drive in the middle of the road, two trucks couldn't pass by each other.

After taking the last ferry to Manaus, I crossed the city and slept near the exit to Boa Vista. I had seven more ferry crossings ahead of me. There were no more bridges.

Further on, in Roraima by now, I got to the Indian reservation, where you have to pass through in groups of two or three trucks. The truck waiting in front of me was lighter than mine, almost empty, it could go a lot faster than me if necessary. But the driver says, 'Hey, Jaú, I've been waiting for you to arrive for two hours, let's go together.' He'd never even seen me before, you know? He was from Goiânia, or Anápoles, and he was joking around, helping me and saying we should drive together. When we'd finished crossing the Indians' land, he went ahead alone, and I followed behind at my own pace.

At six-thirty, seven in the evening, I pulled up at the supermarket in Boa Vista. It was the twenty-third of December.

It was a nice little shop, the best in Boa Vista. The next day was Christmas Eve. The boss told me to park the truck in their lot. 'Tomorrow morning we'll see what to do with your cargo.'

That same day, they got a station wagon with a megaphone on top and they went around the city announcing that wine had arrived in Boa Vista. The wagon went around the whole city until midnight. The next day there was crowds of people there. Within three hours the truck was empty. And only ten flagons had broken.

So I spent Christmas there, at a petrol station. On the twenty-sixth I looked for a little load to take to Manaus, but there was nothing. I went empty-handed, but from there I took cargo to Porto Velho and from Porto Velho to São Paulo. I was on the road for fifty days. Your mother must remember this story, we were dating at the time, I even brought her a present from Boa Vista. Aside from a strong work ethic, traditional masculine honour and pragmatism, truck drivers depended on two other precious resources: companionship and credibility. The ability to rely on the trust of intermediaries, colleagues and petrol station owners was a significant asset, capable of bringing along work opportunities and helping them out of tight spots.

I was carrying a nine-thousand-kilo load of beans to Acre. In Mato Grosso, I entered the Cerrado, a stretch with no highway, so we had to go through the forest itself. After less than one kilometre, the truck hit an ant nest. Ants eat everything from under the earth; it looks normal from above but a hollow forms underneath. When the truck hit that nest, it sank so deep it was completely stuck. We tied it to three, four trucks in front and nothing, it wouldn't budge. We had to grab half of the cargo that was on my truck, lay a tarp down on the floor to keep the beans dry and put half the load on top. That way, with only half a load, those four trucks managed to pull me out of the ant nest. This is how we had to go about it: first, drive until we got to a solid road, then put that half load that was on the truck on the ground, go back to get the one I'd left behind and then return to pick up the rest from the road. It took us a day and a half to get the truck out of the hole.

Drivers who regularly covered a certain stretch and stopped at the same petrol stations got to know one another, even if they saw each other just a few times a year and couldn't communicate between one meeting and the next. These acquaintances, friends on the tarmac, warned each other of dangers on the road, talked about other friends in common and shared job opportunities. And, of course, they were drinking and partying companions too. They were the main source of solace for drivers in the face of a fundamental condition of their work: the long hours of solitude.

Back then, meeting up with your colleagues was the hardest thing in the world, everything was so far away. Sometimes you'd go a whole day without seeing another truck on the road, without a soul to share some thoughts with. But it was nice how every time you happened to pass the truck of someone you knew, we would stop, stand there for ten or fifteen minutes, chatting. Those were good friendships.

It was also crucial to have the trust of petrol station owners and managers. The station on the side of the road was an all-encompassing institution in the lives of these truck drivers: restaurant, bedroom, office, bar, brothel, bathroom, public square, and a centre for communications and business dealings all at once. Experienced drivers nurtured trusting relationships with these proprietors and attendants, which allowed them to open tabs and only pay on the return leg, by which time they would have received the lion's share of the freight.

In many of the stretches in Amazonia, the distance between petrol stations was immense, which meant that the drivers also had to carry part of their own fuel. *On the stretch above Boa Vista, you need to leave São Paulo with a two-hundred-litre drum, as well as the big tank on the truck. There were a lot of ferry crossings, back then there were almost no bridges and one river after another. And we had to carry an axe and a machete in our truck because you always found trees that had fallen on the road, and you had to cut them and drag them away to get past.*

The endless hours were filled with heaps of cigarette packets. Fatty food, sausages, lots of alcohol. Sleepless nights so you could fit in one more journey. Many drivers took *rebite* – a kind of amphetamine that's fairly common on the roads – along with other drugs to stay awake. My father swears he never took *rebite*, snorted cocaine or smoked weed. I don't believe him, but I drop the subject.

At that time, from São Paulo to Belém, six days' travel was normal. And trucks carrying vegetables had to do it in three days; they had seventy-two hours to get from the state supply centre in São Paulo to the central market in Belém, if not it would all rot. They'd go straight through on rebite, *three days and three nights without sleeping. And often they still didn't make it because the road was so crazy.*

The radio on loud so you wouldn't doze off: *There was a stretch of the Trans-Amazonian that was a long line of nearly five hundred kilometres through thick jungle – a tunnel of forest with no petrol stations, no villages, nothing on the road. My greatest fear was that I'd fall asleep, and the truck would flip and smash into a tree, so I turned the radio up to max and sang along, howling out the words so that I'd stay awake, stay safe.*

The hardest time to be away from family was the holiday season, Christmas, Easter, the times when people get together, meet up. I always had a big family. For holidays, everyone would get together at Grandma and Grandpa's house. And then I had you two. However much you want to unwind, that thought always comes along, reminding you that you're far away and your families are at home. There was no alternative, you had to put up with being sad, get used to it. I'd put on my little radio in the cab, listen to a tune that got to me, made me remember my sons and my wife, and then the emotions would surface, the longing, and I'd drive the truck until I got there. That was life.

Truck drivers from my father's generation were physically scarred by the risks, challenges and vices of that world.

70

Many of them were still young when they were first affected by a huge range of ailments – cardiac, vascular,
orthopaedic, hepatic. *Dito? Complete alcoholic, always lying
around drunk, almost died three times from cirrhosis. Valdir
lost both feet from diabetes when he was still a young man.
Aristeu had a stroke, he's been bedridden for a while now. And
Zelão died too, I don't know what from, but he died young.*

My father: heart attack at forty-eight, four bypasses,
one mammary bypass, several catheterizations. Appendicitis at fifty-two, his gall bladder having been
removed decades earlier. Twenty-seven pills spread
out through the day – his extensive pharmacopoeia, as
Barthes called these chemical prostheses that accompany
the sick body wherever it goes. His travelling pharmacy
confuses the nurses forced to adapt to this draconian
regime during his hospital stays (they often give up and
ask me or my brother to administer the pills, breaking the
protocol by which they are meant to abide but increasing
the chances of my father being properly medicated).

A serious case of malaria when he was around thirty:
*I travelled from Rondônia to Jaú trembling with fever, inject-
ing myself with the medicine the pharmacists had sold me in
Porto Velho. I cut off a bit of inner tube from the truck to make
the tourniquet and injected myself. I was hospitalized in Jaú,
they did all the tests and gave me the medicine and I still didn't
improve. They didn't know how to treat malaria here in São
Paulo. I spent nine or ten days there. I was weak, dying, and
they wanted to open me up to see what it was, but I didn't let
them operate, I escaped from the hospital in the middle of the
night. In those days, the exam results took days to arrive but
eventually they confirmed it was malaria. They gave me a
blood transfusion, put me on some medication and I started
to improve.*

The skin on his neck reveals incipient growths that will

need to be removed one day. In 2015, there was another 'minor heart attack', in the cardiologist's words, which left him with three more stents. An artery in his heart remained partially blocked – the doctors decided not to operate, since the risks were too high. He gets terrible cramps in the leg from which arteries were taken for his heart surgery; they often wake him several times during the night.

His shoulders and elbows hurt, gout swells his feet, his left leg sometimes disobeys him. Two immense hernias adorn his abdomen. Sometimes a strange electrical tingle crosses his nose and forehead, inch by inch. Only with his second heart attack, at seventy-two, did he grudgingly agree to retire. And now, cancer.

Among the kinds of knowledge my father acquired over fifty years on the road is a notable skill for organizing loads and volumes. Badly distributed loads on a truck's trailer can lead to tragedy. My father describes an accident he witnessed in western Pará: *I was the first to arrive at the scene of the accident. The driver of the timber truck must have fallen asleep and collided head-on with the bus, on a slope. The logs must have been poorly tied so one went over the trailer, tore the cabin from the truck and went into the bus, coming out at the rear. There were fifty-one people onboard. You could feel the warm blood trickling along the tarmac. Back then, there was only one bus a day or even every two days in those parts, so there were people on top of the baggage rack. That's why the tragedy happened, and only one passenger survived. This guy, the only one who didn't die, went mad and spent his whole life living at a nearby petrol station. People helped him; sometimes he swept the station courtyard, sometimes he did nothing. And the locals put fifty white crosses by the side of the road at the site of the accident. When I went to Pará with your mother, on*

our honeymoon, I took a photo of those crosses, but she threw it
away, she didn't like it.

So it's vital to be able to organize things in their cor-
rect place. The demands of all that cargo has conferred
on him something like an honorary doctorate in applied
geometry. Simply filling a supermarket trolley in front
of my father is a thankless task, since any attempt at
organization is always on the wrong side of the Cartesian
expectations he sets, as if the division of that space
between milk cartons, eggs, vegetables and cleaning products were something upon which the fate of humanity
depended.

Illness, we quickly learn, respects no geometry. It challenges our mental capacity to visualize the paths along
which fluids run, to map the overlay of the organs, to
imagine the internal folds and comprehend the tumour's
limits.

On the computer, the urologist shows us an enormous
mass, 'three times bigger than normal', pressing on the intestines and invading the bladder. This colossal prostate
was squashing the urethra, not allowing the urine to get
to its natural destination. Yet another operation reared its
head, a 'prostate scraping'. The procedure doesn't fix the
bladder, which at this point had become a muscular organ thanks to years of involuntary training to overcome
the blockages imposed by the prostate. My father moves
from a fatal inability to urinate to incontinence, an un-
satisfactory result for a complex engineering of pumps,
reservoirs, canals and fluids in his short body.

His boldly anti-Euclidian form takes on new folds,
orifices, cavities, creases. Shapes worn away by time
or moulded by surgeons' hands. In his sick body, these
twisting pathways, the flaccid vesicles and reddened

73

matter extend beyond him, connecting to bags, channels and catheters, industrial appendices which, configured by our limited Cartesian intelligence, seem so strange when coupled with the body's organic sinuosity. Square adhesives, bags with hermetic closures, rubbery suckers are enlisted in a synthetic attempt to bring order to the visceral and the scatological, to that which belongs to the viscous dimension of the *human*, a dimension that is so familiar to us and yet beyond our ability to verbalize. As if the word could only be summoned when we sign up to the charade that we are not merely intestines, urethras, prostates, urine, skin, hair and shit; as if civilization can only come into existence when we hide these folds and prohibited materials that bring us face to face with our ultimate condition as animals.

From his ankle to his left upper thigh, my father's leg bears the traces from the incisions of several catheterizations and the removal of blood vessels. On his abdomen, scars from the surgery to remove his appendix; the flesh-coloured stoma surrounded by the hideous hernia; an immense pink scar in the middle of his belly, left by a gall bladder operation decades earlier. Another fine, white line divides his chest. He remembers other marks, invisible to external observers: the phimosis operation, the cataract surgery and the internal trajectory of the prostate scraping. From his feet to his throat, the scars delineate the vertical axis of his body, a meridian that cuts him in half, like a road tearing through skin.

IV. NESTOR

The person I travelled with most was a driver from here in Jaú, my friend Nestor. Whenever I needed something on the road, whatever it was, he helped me, and I helped him back. He was a great companion during my first year of travel, when I was learning the job and getting to know the country. We discovered a lot of roads travelling together.

He died young, poor guy. He wasn't even fifty. He's been gone a good while now. I don't know what he died of. There was always something wrong with his health. All I know is, he left us too soon.

It was with him I saw the alien in the north of Mato Grosso, right up at the top, almost on the border with Rondônia.

There was no movement at all on the road, it was pitch black. The night was moonless and there was no light on the road, no towns along the way. Me and Nestor were each in our own trucks.

Halfway through the journey, we start seeing four little moving red lights, in the middle of the forest, skirting the road, like lights from a plane when it's changing direction in the sky. Only, these lights were very low, right above us and going at the same speed. They were trailing us.

Me and Nestor both saw them. My truck was in front. We drove for about half an hour, forty minutes. Eventually, we both stopped and I said, 'Hey Nestor, you seeing this?' 'Yeah, I've been seeing it for a while, I was going to signal at you to stop.' 'But what the hell is it?' 'Well, it's whatever God wills. Let's just keep going.'

We drove a little further until we saw a telephone tower ahead of us. But before we reached it those four lights above us crossed over to the opposite side of the road and stopped. Must have been about a hundred metres away. The same distance it had been from us on the left side, it crossed and went over to our right. And stopped. Nestor was now in front and I stopped my truck about twenty metres behind him.

We got out and looked around. By the time we stopped it wasn't just the lights any more: there was also a noise, like a very strong wind or the sound of a welding machine.

'My God, what the hell is it?'

We were stuck to the spot, just looking at the lights, talking to each other – scared. And that was when we saw a figure emerging from the lights and coming towards us.

'Look at the shape! Are you seeing it, are you seeing the shape, Nestor?'

It looked like a man in a long cape, walking in our direction. Nestor jumps into his truck, 'Come on, let's get out of here.' He jumps in and drives off, his truck was right by where we were, but for me, running those twenty metres to my truck, oh boy... It felt like I ran for a day and still wasn't reaching it. I thought this thing was going to get me, take me away.

We shot off in our trucks. The lights followed us for a bit and then vanished. The lights went out and we never saw them again... Not the figure or the lights or the sound. It ended in nothing.

—

We drove and drove until we got to the village near the tower at three-thirty in the morning. We parked our trucks and slept.

At the village, we found out that stretch was famous for being haunted.

The next day, we spoke to a guy at the local bar, and he told us lots of people had died on that road in cars, buses... There were even crosses right there on the side of the road. Just recently, a Japanese guy was driving with his wife and kid, and he crashed and they all died.

He said this stretch had a ghost which appeared and frightened the drivers. But I don't think so. It wasn't haunted, there was no ghost there.

I'll never know what it was I saw.

Later, I talked a fair bit with people who understand these things and they think it was an extraterrestrial. In fact, the person who spoke to me and confirmed it was an alien was Father Luiz. I told him the story the way I'm telling you now and he said: 'There's no doubt it was an alien that was following you.'

Such a shame my friend Nestor is dead. If he was alive, he'd tell the story just as I'm telling it.

It was Nestor who taught me about exhaust barbecue. Above the truck's exhaust there's a plate that gets red hot. This is inside the engine, not the pipe where the smoke comes out. It's a part that's attached to the engine, welded metal, concave, big enough for one or two kilos of meat. You'd tie a piece of meat there in the morning and when you stopped at midday the barbecue would be ready. It was delicious, so good. Or you'd make the food at lunch and fill a pot with food for dinner, but at night you didn't need to light a fire, just open the truck's bonnet, put the pot there, leave it on top of the exhaust which had been heating up all day. Then you could shower at the petrol station, have a few drinks, come back to get the pot and it was piping hot. That was life.

He started driving earlier than me; he was a bit older, Nestor. Uncle Nerso died, Nestor died, Jaques died. Laércio too, he died from drinking too much. He drank at home, at the bar, in his truck. He drank and drank and drank.

From that whole group of friends, I think only me and two others are left.

V. KILLING AND KILLING

'I want my opera house! I want my opera house!
This church remains closed until this town has
its opera house!'
—— Werner Herzog, *Fitzcarraldo*

At three in the afternoon on 19 August 2019, it was no longer possible to see the sunlight in São Paulo. I was discussing *The Eighteenth Brumaire of Louis Bonaparte* with my students – Karl Marx's classic essay in which he analyzes how different groups of common people and reactionary elites were mobilized by a leader, until then seen as stupid and vulgar, to establish an authoritarian government in December 1851. It's at the start of this book that Marx presents his celebrated idea that all the events and characters in history are staged twice, 'first as tragedy, then as farce'.

If Marx had been with me and wished to illustrate his thesis on the repetition of history, he could have simply asked the students to look out of the window: a dark, dirty cloud was sullying the São Paulo sky. Like the Benjaminian angel of history, the grey monster was inviting us to look at the ashes of the past and our foolish insistence on restaging our catastrophe in ever more tragic ways. That sombre blanket was the exaggeratedly oracular incarnation of our dismal present and our history of devastation. The result of a season of criminal fires in Amazonia and the country's mid-west region, the cloud condensed the accelerated destruction of the forests, the socio-environmental crimes that were only becoming more common, seas of waste carrying away entire villages, mercury poisoning of indigenous Amazonian people and a presidential election that had recast tragedy as a cause for celebration.

In the grey São Paulo sky, the tragedy of the past was fused with the authoritarian farce of the present, pointing towards a future of ruins.

The first memories I have of the Amazon rainforest, its rivers and roads, indigenous people and ribeirinhos come from my father's stories. Narratives of his travels through the region helped me to compose my infant vocabulary, my sentimental geography, the mythology of a travelling father and a country that seemed infinite.

To drive a truck in the Amazon, back when they were opening it all up, you had to be an adventurer. Restaurants and markets were almost non-existent, just the roadside stalls. The tastiest food they would have there would be tapioca flour. And there was lots of fish, dried fish, every kind of fish. There was lots of bush meat. Paca, armadillo, coati, deer, anaconda meat; those were the kinds of things we ate. The company building the road had a hunting team whose job was to gather food for people to eat so they could work. At that time lots of people were starting to arrive from the south, from Mato Grosso and from the north-east, but it increased a lot once the road was ready. Then you really saw people coming.

The Trans-Amazonian Highway (BR-230), a megalomaniac project to connect the Atlantic and Pacific oceans by land, promised to elevate the country to a position of greatness at the start of the 1970s. The nearly-four-thousand-kilometre-long road, running from east to west, would cross six states, from the Atlantic north-east to the border with Peru, promising to be the great corridor through which north-eastern workers would arrive and from which wood, gold, cattle and agricultural products cultivated on deforested land would leave.

When I was a child, I thought of the Trans-Amazonian Highway as 'my dad's road'.

These immense infrastructural projects first drew breath in the early 1970s, the bloodiest period of the dictatorship then led by General Médici. The government heralded the Trans-Amazonian as the miraculous fulfilment of a programme of national engineering. This would guarantee the occupation of the northern region in accordance with the Doctrine of National Security, promoting the rapid development of the country, protecting against foreign invaders and offering a solution to the poverty and rural tensions of the north-east.

In the language of the time, the colossal undertaking would link the north-east's 'men with no land' to the rainforest's 'land with no men'. It was necessary to occupy, to penetrate the 'green inferno', 'integrate not abdicate'. Médici described the road's construction as 'the greatest adventure any people on the face of the earth have ever lived through'. At the inauguration of one of the stretches in 1972, the then minister of transport, Mário Andreazza, professed: 'Finally, Amazonia is populated. Brazil is broadening. The country has greater magnitude and its children more faith in their own destinies.'

The highways were the spearhead of this aggressive endeavour, my father one of the thousands of workers occupied with its construction. He transported stone, sand, gravel, basic items and provisions for construction workers as well as the soldiers who oversaw their work. The sad opera of progress in that ravaged Amazonia was staged by chainsaws and machine-guns, land-grabbers and mercenaries, truck drivers and small farmers in search of land and work, contracted workers, poor people from the region itself and other corners of the country

– the many different faces of the wretched of our land in the service of 'the great business of the nation'.

By the end of the sixties there was already a lot of logging, but it was only after more roads were opened up that the timber business really exploded. When I was travelling through Acre in the sixties and seventies, all you saw was convoys of timber trucks. No one ever talked about conserving the forest, you never heard any of that. Cherry, mahogany, chestnut... In those streams you could count two hundred logs bobbing along, one tied to the other; they would float down the river until they could be transported on a truck.

To workers attracted by these expanding frontiers, the destruction of the forest was sold as an inevitable path towards collective progress and a dignified life. Many of them ended up settling there, minor pawns in the process of deforestation and the occupation of government lands. Others formed the outskirts of cities that were beginning to expand; impoverished urban nuclei whose economies depend to this day on predatory acts of environmental exploitation, prospecting and a whole host of activities on the fringes of the law.

Every town we passed through had a sawmill by the side of the road. We transported lots of hardwood timber. My brother Nerso almost only did jobs carrying wood from here to there; I did a few myself. Even back then I thought it was destructive. I had a feeling it was no good, but at the time no one talked about it, they thought the forest would never end. It was all incentivized and we had to make a living.

My father crossed the Araguaia region dozens of times in the early 1970s. There, between south-eastern Pará and Tocantins, the dictatorship pursued young revolutionaries and local peasants in one of the bloodiest chapters of Brazilian military rule. Inspired by the Cuban and Chinese revolutions, these young militants mostly came from the south and south-east of the country. The peasants called them *paulistas* or 'students'.

This was a region of small farmers, mostly poor migrants from the north-east, who had settled there to escape from the poverty and oppression of the countryside. In their places of origin their enemies were 'drought and fences'. Otávio Velho, in his classic study on the frontiers of expansion in the Amazonia in the 1950s and 1960s, points to the way this mass of poor, landless peasants saw geographical mobility as the chance to escape from what they called 'captivity': work for which you receive nothing in exchange, under the political command of landowners in north-eastern and central Brazil. These conditions harked back to the captivity of slavery and made their material and symbolic continuation apparent in the lives of these populations.

In Amazonia, the outsiders founded towns and cities with biblical names, a succession of Canaans, Promised Lands and New Jerusalems. The majority of these north-eastern migrants in the 1960s and early 1970s settled in these territories with no support from the government or any other patrons. This would change somewhat in the coming years, when the federal government created some official 'settlement' programmes which attracted new waves of rural migrants, many of them from the south, seduced by a series of benefits and fiscal incentives.

The Araguaia guerrilla war, which took place in the vicinity of the recently opened Trans-Amazonian Highway, was another stage for the dictatorship's sadistic theatre, ramped up by the Institutional Act 5 of 1968.

Of the nearly eight hundred fighters, only twenty or so survived the incursions of thousands of soldiers in successive military offensives between 1972 and 1974.

Many of the local farmers in Araguaia, with no political connection to the young people who opposed the regime, were victims of the same violence. Witnesses of this official brutality attest that electricity first reached the region in the form of the loose wires used by the military during their torture sessions.

Truck drivers lived alongside soldiers on these frontiers of expansion. In their day-to-day encounters, camaraderie sometimes gave way to confrontation, and authority did not always lie with the other side.

We were on our way from Porto Velho to São Paulo, carrying cargo. We got to Pimenta Bueno, in Rondônia, and the road was closed off. There was a mudhole so big that no one could pass, not even the army's jeeps. The soldiers put two tractors on the dirt track, to block the way, and there was a huge queue of trucks wanting to pass. I was fifth in line.

It rained night and day and we were just sitting there. It didn't stop.

That queue of trucks was stuck there for four days. There were more than a hundred trucks. The fifth day arrived and what did we decide? We'll cross tomorrow. There's no other way. Most of us agreed. There were only two soldiers at that post and two tractors blocking the track. There was no way of passing with those vehicles there.

There was a driver, Paulão, and he said to me: 'Jaú, if I move the machine, will you pass?' I said I would.

He went and moved one of the tractors from the middle of the road. Then me, Joel, Jaques, Bastião, Catarina and Goiânia all passed. Six trucks passed.

Then all hell broke loose.

*One of the soldiers jumped onto the truck and put his re-
volver to my head. 'Stop or I'll kill you! Stop or I'll kill you!'
And I said, 'You won't kill anything, you don't have the courage, look at all the drivers behind me.' And he didn't shoot. He
jumped down from the truck and stayed on the road watching
the others pass. And we passed.*

*We worked for four days and four nights without stopping,
until we'd crossed fifty kilometres of boggy land.*

*But then I had a word with the other five who had crossed
before me: 'Let's be quick, 'cause when we get to Vila Rondon
we're gonna get the shit kicked out of us; get ready for a beat-
ing, jail or worse.' There was another army camp there. We
crossed the mudhole and arrived. The commandant at the military post asked, all puffed up: 'Was this what you wanted?' I
said, 'Well, the soldiers at the post were doing nothing, so we
decided to handle it ourselves. We know how to drive through
mudholes. You just need to grab buckets wherever there are
holes, fill them with stones, close up the hole and drive past.
One truck tugs another if needed. That was our only intention,
so that's what we did and now we're here and ready to continue the journey.' There was a pause, and then he said: 'Then
go with God and may God bless you, may you always have such
courage in your work.'*

*The five of us all clapped with joy and relief, see, because
we thought we were going to be stuck there or that they'd get
rid of us...*

Zé, you always say you're on the left, but what does that mean?
he asked me recently when he heard me cursing some
politician on the TV.

Even though he spent several years of his life on the
colossal building sites that functioned as postcards for
the authoritarian regime, my father rarely talks about the
dictatorship. This word is absent from the many hours of

our conversations, as if it had been in some way negated.

I cannot name the Brazil that emerges through his stories using my academic vocabulary. Almost none of my father's words square with the narrative critical of the authoritarian regime recorded in the books I read as a student, researcher and professor. Neither does his discourse align itself with a kind of vainglorious thinking, with reactionary praise of the military-led regime. I get tied up when I try to dress his speech in the glossary of the enlightened, progressive political debate I am accustomed to.

These critical accounts did not reach him in a way that made any sense or shed any light on his experiences, nor did they suggest other ways of telling his and his country's story. When he recalls the financial backers behind the military regime, he mentions the enormous machines that opened colossal furrows in the coastal mountains, or the times he met *Mr Camargo Correa, who was also from Jaú,* inspecting building projects and cursing the waste of parts he saw thrown around on the ground. If he brings up soldiers, he's referring to concrete individuals that he met in some corner of the country, like the soldiers he transported to Santarém in his trailer in the early 1970s, on a recently opened stretch of road that took days to cross.

Sometimes he remembers that *we used to be scared of even saying the word 'president'.* But he can't describe where this fear came from, nor does he draw any great conclusions from it. In my father's stories, there is no Marighella, no Golbery, and the battles he witnessed did not take place in Rua Maria Antônia or Cinelândia Square.

All that torture and repression stuff, we heard about it from time to time, but I never saw any of it on the road. When I ask if he remembers the dictatorship's propaganda about the Trans-Amazonian Highway, the 'colonization' of the northern region, the way the military promised to bring 'progress' to these regions, the guerrilla war in Araguia and other instances of resistance to the regime, his answers are always brief: *I wouldn't know what to say about that.* Or: *No, I don't remember that.*

Amazonia continues to be a huge unknown in the rest of the country, an internal Belgian Congo at the service of the perverse fantasies of an urban, coastal King Leopold. The region is the great physical and symbolic victim of this Brazilian version of orientalism, the Trans-Amazonian Highway one of the clumsy attempts to realize the secular dream of 'colonizing' the immense forest, together with other forms of occupation: the rubber cycle in the nineteenth century, the Madeira-Mamoré train track at the beginning of the twentieth century, the Belém-Brasília highway in the 1950s, the endless predation of the present.

Flávio Gomes, a journalist invited by the military government to document the construction works, illustrates this military-orientalist imagination which the highway inspired:

> There, in the deep heart of the jungle, a country that was until recently very poor is succeeding in establishing a civilization. A new frontier is being opened, with the pioneer spirit, faith and – most importantly – joy and good humour. And there shall always be a solid, definitive border, imprinting our sovereignty on another Brazil, which until recently only existed on a map and in the avarice of foreigners. The lesson we are learning, one which filled me with pride and patriotism and convinced me that old Médici is right after all – is that no one controls this country.

In the colonizer's view, Amazonia and its peoples are the heart of darkness, and the highway is the river down which civilization (and lucre) must flow. The forest and its peoples become obstacles in a funeral march of progress driven by tractors, trucks, oxen, chainsaws, dust. As Heidegger foresaw, 'The hydroelectric plant is not built into the Rhine River as was the old wooden bridge that joined bank with bank for hundreds of years. Rather the river is dammed up into the power plant.' The forest is dammed up into the highway, this living monument to our catastrophes.

A 1971 advertisement by the military government incentivized the migration of cattle ranchers to Amazonia, promising public subsidies and endless land. The main slogan was 'Drive your cattle to the greatest pasture in the world.'

To make the roads, they cut the forest down with chainsaws, pushed the trees on each side onto the conveyor belts, gradually forming a path through it. Every five or six kilometres there was a stream or a small river. One after the other. We'd go into the water and come out the other side. In many of them there were already some footbridges: they'd throw down some reinforced logs, screwing one to the other. To get to the other side, you had to risk going over. We carried everything: construction materials, but also things for the company workers: typewriters, chairs, paper, dry food, toilet paper, all sorts. There was a time when we almost always took timber back with us on the return journey, see? To São Paulo, Rio, Campinas, the port of Santos, wherever the sawmill told you to go. Hardwood, for making furniture. They managed to destroy everything there. There's only pasture left.

I am reminded of Carlos Drummond de Andrade,

another narrator of our collapse. In his work, the immense iron machines that razed the outskirts of the Itabira of his childhood march inexorably past. Drummond makes poetry out of the concrete material of the surrounding mountains in Minas Gerais, those hills that depart 'on the monster-train of five locomotives', leaving their cursed mining dust in both the body and the landscape.

Our history of development, a continental accumulation of pasture and dust.

A vast portion of that highway was transformed into a muddy corridor along which wood and minerals travelled, as well as soya, eucalyptus, oxen, contraband products, narcotics.

Starting from the highways, settlers and ranchers open up smaller roads which penetrate deeper and deeper into the forest, forming a structure akin to a fish's spine, and enlarging the region of deforestation produced by the road's construction. The trails and backroads in continual expansion invade conservation units, unoccupied land and indigenous territories and quilombos that should enjoy the protection of government power. This system of roads, big and small, makes up the corridors through which the destruction and burning of the world's largest tropical rainforest – the biggest storehouse of biodiversity on the planet and one of the main guarantors of climatic regulation on Earth – is perpetrated. São Felix do Xingu, in southern Pará, is now the city with the country's highest rates of greenhouse gas emissions thanks to deforestation and extensive cattle ranching. Alone, this city jammed in the middle of Amazonia contributes more to global warming than the whole of Chile.

Destruction always plays out according to the same script: it generally starts with hardwood trees being cut down. This is followed by more widespread razing and burning of forest to create pastures for extensive cattle rearing. The presence of oxen or low-productivity agriculture favours land-grabbing, or benefits the illegal occupiers embroiled in long disputes for their ownership of land yet to be regularized – disputes that are often sponsored by ranchers, entrepreneurs and politicians. In contrast to what was believed for a long time, much of the Amazonian soil is fertile because of the forest; without it, it degrades and becomes unsuitable for agriculture within a very short amount of time. During the initial years of exploitation, the region in question tends to see rapid economic growth, spurred by the profits from these illegal activities, but this dynamism rarely generates any development beyond the initial spoiling of the forest and the soil.

The deforesters then abandon these areas and go further into the forest, where a new cycle of devastation begins. Behind them remain barren lands and impoverished villages, a pattern of occupation that the researcher Adalberto Veríssimio called 'boom-collapse'. The vast majority of the eighty-three million deforested hectares – almost twenty per cent of the rainforest's territory – consists either of underused or completely degraded land. Close to these corridors of deforestation there tends to be illegal prospecting, trafficking of drugs and minerals, predatory hunting and fishing, child prostitution and the brutalization of traditional people and their lands.

Indigenous territories, *quilombos* and extractive reserves are ever more frequently the targets of incursion by land-grabbers, loggers, miners and their powerful patrons: mayors, MPs, police chiefs, notaries, drug traffickers, lawyers and large-scale landowners. These human and environmental tragedies go almost unnoticed by the elites in the big cities of the country's south and south-east, delighted with the seat they have been given at the cynical feast of the global economy, this ancient marriage between shamelessness and devastation which sets the tone for our history.

Out there they had this saying: kill one man and tie the other one up for the next day...

One time, in Maranhão: it was around midnight when we got to a village, it was a swamp. A wooden bridge came off the road and went fifty metres into the forest. At the entrance there was a small bar. We always went in for coffee, dinner or lunch; it was a stopping point for truck drivers. Anyway, I said: 'Nestor, shall we go and grab something?' 'Let's go.' There was a lamp tied to the trunk in the middle of the shack, which had a thatched roof.

We went up to the counter to order a coffee. That was when I looked out the back and saw a guy tied to a trunk. I drank my coffee, then I asked the man at the bar: 'You saving that one for tomorrow?' and he said, 'No, nothing like that. He was causing a fuss, fighting and drinking, so the other guys tied him up. I'll let him go soon.' That's what he said, and we left not long after. Really though, who knows what happened to the poor guy.

Altamira, Pará state, the 'Princess of the Xingu', frequently occupies the highest spot in the national murder rate rankings. This is where the Belo Monte hydroelectric dam, the third largest in the world, was inaugurated in 2011. The plant is the final realization of a project initially rolled out in 1974, at the height of the military dictatorship. The colossal concrete monster caused the flooding of indigenous lands, destroyed the local people's traditional fishing practice, and increased the persecution and killing of its local leadership and the aggravation

93

of bloody disputes between drug cartels. In one episode from this continual war, in 2019, sixty-two prisoners were killed during a massacre that lasted for five hours in the city's jail. Sixteen of the victims were decapitated. Images of their lacerated bodies travelled around the country via WhatsApp.

The city also became known as the 'capital of the Trans-Amazonian Highway'. From the 1960s onwards, Altamira was a laboratory for all the perverse variations of the ideology of progress, and fantasies of development were already present in the region before the highway was built.

I took cane up to Altamira. This was in '65, just after I'd started working in a truck. I loaded up the cane seeds in Sertãozinho, which is near Jaú. They were building a plant in Altamira, but they didn't have enough road to get there. The Trans-Amazonian Highway came later. Before that, we had to go to Belém, and once we were there I put the truck on the ferry and it carried us to near where they were building the plant. Only we didn't even take our trucks off the ferry: the plant's trucks came with their tractors, took the cargo from our trucks, passed them over to the plant's trucks and took seeds to be planted. When they finished building the plant, the farmland was already complete. I saw a piece of the field around the time the construction work on the Trans-Amazonian started. Because I was in the area I drove past Altamira, and there you could see the cane plantations in the middle of all that forest.

It was this city that Médici visited on 9 October 1970 to mark the start of the building of the highway. Images of the president inaugurating a boundary stone for the construction works and taking part in the destruction of a Brazil nut tree were transmitted to television sets throughout the country. That tree's trunk is still there, with a plaque next to it saying: 'On these banks of the

94

River Xingu, in the middle of the Amazon rainforest, the President of the Republic inaugurated the building of the Trans-Amazonian Highway, in a historic leap towards the conquest and colonization of this enormous green world.'

The film *Iracema: An Amazonian Trance*, by Jorge Bodanzky and Orlando Senna, released in 1974, is an allegory for the empty promises of the highway. *Iracema* boldly defied the dictatorship's propaganda in the early 1970s. From its launch, the film circulated clandestinely in the country's film clubs and universities and would only be officially released in Brazilian cinemas in 1980, after six years of censorship by the military regime.

The main character in the film is a popular incarnation of the military dictatorship's developmentalism: 'Tião Brasil Grande', an ambitious, womanizing truck driver from the south of the country, brilliantly played by Paulo César Pereio. Tião is motivated by the hope of getting rich and the belief that his work and his skill and expertise will guarantee this destiny. He synthesizes the dictatorship's promises of a 'Great Brazil', staged in a strategic landscape: Amazonia as it is torn apart by the monstrous highway.

In one scene, Tião lays out the ontology of our capitalism of devastation: 'Nature ain't nobody's mother! Nature's my truck, nature's the road!'

The scenes in the film, described by its directors as a fictional documentary, are almost all improvised, and the majority of the actors are amateurs, local to the region, especially the titular Iracema herself, played by Edna de Cássia. Iracema is a character with whom the protagonist has a relationship that is characterized by diverse forms of violence – prostitution of minors, exploitation of poverty, emotional manipulation, abandonment. Iracema is the representation of so many real Amazonian women, but also an allegory for the forest itself, violated by its process of occupation.

In an almost prophetic fashion, Tião begins the film transporting wood to São Paulo and ends it transporting cattle to Acre. This twist in the character's trajectory concretizes the transformation of the fundamental vector of deforestation operating to this day.

The film's dusty aesthetic, and Tião's clothes – shirts open down to his belly, old T-shirts advertising the building of the highway, chains around his neck, aviator shades and flares – remind me of the few existing photos of my father on the road.

The highway tore apart the territories of twenty-nine indigenous groups, provoking massacres, expulsions, child prostitution and the vandalization of millennia-old cultures. Even the political narratives most critical towards the Brazilian dictatorship say little about the indigenous genocide led by the dictatorship and the civil complex that supported it. According to the Truth Commission, almost eight thousand indigenous people were wiped out in that period, and none of them have a space in the dominant versions of our national history, fed by a miserably urban, white, coastal and south-eastern imagination.

The cities, small towns and rural zones that began to form in the trail of prospecting, deforestation, cattle ranching and land-grabbing always occupy the bottom of our economic and social development rankings. The region's homicide rate is sixty per cent higher than in the rest of the country, and that of youth unemployment almost double.

An alarming proportion of the murders of activists

and other victims of rural and forest conflicts are concentrated in the northern region of Brazil. Landless farmers, indigenous people and human rights defenders are mown down by ranchers, loggers, miners and the landowners who give the local police their orders.

Back then, sixties, seventies, the invaders went on murder sprees. Land-grabbers, prospectors... Killing just to see the other man fall; killing and killing. In Sapucaia, Pará, this one guy had a ranch which was on stolen land. The same guy owned the gas station, the restaurant, rented out a few small rooms there, a little guesthouse. A mercenary arrived and shot him in the face with a twelve-gauge shotgun, took the man's head clean off. I'd just arrived, they only talked about it in the city, but it happened all the time.

It was in these outskirts that the military police killed nineteen landless agrarian workers in 1996, in what became known as the 'Eldorado dos Carajás massacre'. Images of the bloody bodies and the piles of anonymous corpses plastered across the newspapers are one of my oldest memories of Brazilian state violence, mowing down lives indiscriminately.

A little to the north, in the city of Anapu, the North American missionary Sister Dorothy Strang was killed by six bullets in 2005. Her murder was carried out on the orders of local ranchers who had for some time been threatening her because of her work defending the forest and local small farmers. Many rural workers in the region keep photographs of Sister Dorothy on their home altars along with crucifixes and images of saints.

And Pedro Paulino Guajajara, a twenty-six-year-old indigenous man and defender of the forest, was killed by loggers in Maranhão; like so many other indigenous people, from so many different communities, on so many lands, for so, so many years.

The woman of God, the landless and the legions of dead indigenous leaders were joined by the indigenist Bruno Pereira and the journalist Dom Phillips in June 2022, executed near the Javari valley for defending the forest and its original people.

Like the trees, the bodies in the Amazon will not stop falling.

Every society contributes to the universal history of barbarism with its own particular collection of debris. Svetlana Alexievich, reflecting on the place of the Chernobyl disaster, suggests:

> Everything we know of horror and dread is connected primarily with war. Stalin's Gulags and Auschwitz were recent gains for evil. History has always been the story of wars and military commanders, and war was, we could say, the yardstick of horror ... Reports on Chernobyl in the newspapers are thick with the language of war: 'nuclear', 'explosion', 'heroes'. And this makes it harder to appreciate that we now find ourselves on a new page of history. The history of disasters has begun.

In fact, war is not the only yardstick of horror. For Brazil, as in many other societies, it was never the fundamental source of words and memories from which our encyclopaedia of brutality is composed. Our disasters have other names – colonization, genocide, slavery, racism, environmental devastation. Its instruments are the highway, the fence, disease, slave ships, the bullet, the axe, the 'bush captains' – free men hired to hunt down and return escaped slaves, perhaps our first middle-class profession of the colonial period.

Those captains followed one after another all the way

to the present day, with different uniforms and variations on the same sadistic whims – sometimes, certainly, resorting to perversities that echo and reimagine other genocides, such as the makeshift gas chamber in which Genivaldo de Jesus was asphyxiated in May 2022, when two officers locked him inside a police car in Umbaúba, Sergipe, as passers-by – and the rest of the nation – watched on.

Cancer also works according to a colonial logic. It occupies territories that don't belong to it, feeds off living matter and, if left to its own devices, kills the host and then dies along with him. When talking about cancer we use words like 'growth', 'expansion', 'colonization', spatial metaphors for an illness that is the true epic of the occupation of the body's territory, a biological *Fitzcarraldo* that we are all capable of producing as part of our own process of growth, curing, cellular regeneration, life – and which is, at the same time, the second most common cause of death in the world.

Siddhartha Mukherjee, in his history of this 'emperor of all maladies', explains that in the case of cancer there is no single illness. 'Cancer' is just a catch-all category for an immense diversity of similar phenomena of uncontrolled cellular growth. Resuming Douglas Weinberg and Robert A. Hanahan's canonical studies, the author enumerates the six fundamental steps of carcinogenic formation: the activation of accelerators of cellular multiplication; the deactivation of the brakes on multiplication; the evasion of programmed cell death, common in healthy cells (producing the cancerous cell's impetus towards immortality); the infinite potential to keep replicating themselves; the ability to obtain blood and nutrients, the fuel for their expansion; skilfully travelling around the body and taking root in other organs and tissues. This last step is the motor of metastasis, a word that I was not able to pronounce for months and which, in my journal, I called 'the M-word'.

The M-word: according to Mukherjee, metastasis means something like 'beyond stillness': 'an unmoored, partially unstable state that captures the particular instability of modernity ... Cancer is an expansionist disease; it invades through tissues, sets up colonies in hostile landscapes, seeking "sanctuary" in one organ and then immigrating to another.' Like the devastation of the rainforest, cancer is the embodiment of the gospel of growth at any cost.

VI. MANELÃO

*Back then, we'd load the truck, come home, stay a day or two
and then leave again.*

*We were all single, so we'd always pay a visit to the whore-
house before leaving. We'd have some drinks, go with one
woman, go with another, that sort of thing.*

*This one time, it was me, my friend Nestor and Manelão.
And there was a gorgeous blonde there, her name was Helena.
I think she was the prettiest girl in town in those days. And
Helena was getting cheeky with Manelão. She asked where we
were going and we said we were heading for Manaus – and she
said she'd go with us.*

*Manelão replied: 'If you want to come with me, I'll take you,
but you need money, you can't go without money. Food's expensive, everything on the road is expensive.' That was the excuse
he gave to stop her coming...*

*This girl looked him in the eye, put her hands on her
waist and said: 'Money's the problem, is it? Wait here then.'
She walked out into the yard, where there were some of those
five-litre flagons piled up on the floor. Whatever money she
earned, she'd roll it up and throw it into that flagon of hers. She
couldn't even say how much money there was inside.*

*Helena puts her hand on her flagon, goes up to the bar, in
the middle of all the people there, and smashes the flagon on
the floor.*

*It smashed into pieces. Notes, coins and shards of glass all
over the place. 'If it's money you want, then here you go.'*

Manelão said: 'Now you're talking, Helena, let's go!'

*His eyes lit up when he saw her money. He was no good, a
real crook...*

*She did end up going with Manelão. They must have done forty
journeys together. They got married, had a kid... They stayed*

together, but they fought like cat and dog the whole time. They smacked and hit each other, everyone would talk about it. They were both so jealous. After hitting each other they'd laugh about it and get wasted together.

I don't think they're still married because he got sick in the head. Manelão grew old and crazy. He still wanders around the city, doesn't say a word to no one. He wanders aimlessly along the street, with that distant gaze in his eyes. It must be all the drink, all the drugs. Or just pure badness.

I don't know what became of Helena. She must've run away from him.

Manelão was a brute, a real grifter. He was always wheeling and dealing and liked to trick people. Once he bought a monkey, a tame monkey, on the roadside in Acre. At the time they were everywhere, those wild animal traffickers selling by the roadside. But the animal he bought was only placid because it was drunk. When it sobered up, the monkey began to attack Manelão inside the truck cabin. The poor creature wanted to get out at any cost. Manelão took out his revolver and shot the monkey twice inside the cabin, then tossed the animal's body out of the window.

I was driving behind him. I remember, later on, seeing the animal's blood splattered across the cabin, the two bullet holes in the seat.

He also liked to con people, take advantage. Back then when we were all young, the country people when they came into the city would tie their horses to a lamp post and come into the bar to have a shot. Once I was in a bar in the town down the road, on the riverbank; the farmer who was also drinking in there came out of the pub and couldn't find his filly. 'Where's my horse?' he shouted. Manelão had taken the kid's mare and was trotting around the city, showing off.

He'd come to a bar, open the cash register and take the money right in front of them. He'd steal a boat motor in Pará and sell it in São Paulo... And he was always swindling other drivers, that kind of thing.

None of the other drivers trusted him. But when I was having heart surgery, he came to visit three or four times. No one visited me more than him. If Manelão was right in the head, he'd definitely love to have you over and tell you our stories. A friend is a friend, that's something I'll never forget.

'"Alas," said the mouse, "the whole world is growing smaller every day. At the beginning it was so big that I was afraid, I kept running and running, and I was glad when I saw walls far away to the right and left, but these long walls have narrowed so quickly that I am in the last chamber already, and there in the corner stands the trap that I must run into."

"You only need to change your direction," said the cat, and ate it up.'
—— Franz Kafka, 'A Little Fable'

In May 2018, my father and I watched in shock as truck drivers nationwide came to a historic standstill. At dozens of strategic points across the whole of Brazil, truck drivers crossed their arms, stopped delivering cargo and blocked their colleagues from passing, bringing the country to the brink of a collapse in supply and a serious political crisis. We spoke over the phone about the road blockades which were increasing hourly over those ten days. As in June 2013, these hours turned into weeks, and we seemed to be losing the ability to name things.

The strike was sparked by successive increases in the price of diesel, but new demands from the truck drivers came and went at the same speed at which short-lived leaders entered and exited the scene. At the blockade points we couldn't see any flags representing political parties, organized social movements or unions.

Many of the truck drivers were chanting against corruption, echoing the slogans and feelings that had spread across the country years ago. Some of the left described the protests as a 'lockout', a plot by the bosses and not an autonomous and legitimate workers' protest. The absence of obvious leaders and representative organizations – such a familiar phenomenon on the public stage in recent years – made the demonstrators' messages even harder to organize according to any distinct political programme.

Journalists, politicians, academics, political commentators: we were all stumbling over events and choking on our own theories.

Some of the truck drivers were asking for the return of the military while others stated that they would vote for left-wing candidates. Some radical voices took part in these agitations, trying to take advantage of the upheaval to promote an extreme right-wing programme. One of them, Ramiro Cruz, the coordinator of Despertar da Consciência Patriótica [Patriotic Consciousness Awakening] and an activist who favours the military's return to power, shouted on his Facebook page:

> Victory is close! Truck drivers + The People x Legality x Legitimacy = Fall of the Brazilian Bastille!!! Don't let up, let the National Security Force and the rest of them come, this is the frontline and we won't retreat a single millimetre, because we are the people and the people are united.

Other drivers told journalists and researchers they didn't really care about politics and just wanted to be able to take money home at the end of each month.

The two of us reflected on that series of events with equal interest but from very different starting points. I thought using words I had learnt in books: class, precariousness, historical subject, democracy, co-optation, consciousness. He thought with other ones, rooted in his practical life: freight, cargo, petrol, transportation, boss, taxes, toll.

Who were these people? Heroes of the working class, the pawns of transportation entrepreneurs, the vanguard of a new protofascist movement? How were they organizing? I came up with questions similar to those asked by the academic left to which I belong, mostly arising from our failure to listen to an almost non-existent dialogue with members of the working classes – the typical aversion of the elites towards understanding workers on their own terms, rather than as projections of our concepts, theories and visions of the world.

The elites of the academic and political left – the vast majority of them white, male and economically privileged – tend to impose a cruel form of paternalist censorship on the working classes. Didier Eribon, in *Return to Reims*, highlights one origin of this political, social and epistemic distancing with great precision:

> For me, the 'proletariat' was an idea that came straight out of a book, something abstract. My parents didn't fit the image ... [T]his 'revolutionary' political position simply served as a cover for the social judgment that I had passed on my parents and my family, for my desire to escape from their world.

To project our abstract concepts onto groups of people is a defence mechanism against actually including them in the political debate and in elite cultural institutions. Instead of silencing them with weapons and censorship, we often shut them up with hermetic ideas and self-absorbed institutions that protect us from a movement based around real dialogue. Exceptions to this pattern are rare, and generally happen in spaces that people who come from those social groups have had to struggle to gain access to.

Who are all these people? How did they manage to bring them all together? What do they want? This never happened in my day.

My father's surprise during those ten days also revealed the distance between himself and the current reality of those workers. This was no longer the universe he used to inhabit, and the truck drivers blockading the highways were not Nestor, Manelão or Jaques. The drivers we saw on the TV use WhatsApp to exchange political memes and to communicate with comrades and family. They find work on mobile apps, not just at stands by the roadside or at cargo delivery posts, negotiated through middlemen known as *gatos*, or cats. They face the far more serious risk of being the victims of assaults and kidnapping; this means that their trucks must be equipped with countless security apparatuses and satellite tracking that did not exist a few decades ago. Many of them are armed, which was also common on the roads of the 1960s and 1970s. They are members of a category that remains predominantly male, despite a minor increase in the number of female truck drivers and a far more pronounced presence of feminist discourse in society.

The consumption of stimulant drugs remains commonplace among drivers, but the traditional *rebite* coexists with other amphetamines, as well as cocaine and performance enhancement medications such as Ritalin and Vyvanse. Alcoholism, smoking and heart conditions are still very common, with an alarming rise in the diagnosis of anxiety and depression disorders among members of the category.

Most still nurse the dream of becoming transportation entrepreneurs. Truck drivers are a kind of vanguard of neoliberal ambition, one that converts workers into small-scale entrepreneurs lacking any rights or guarantees. Any risk these workers take on is private, and surprises they meet on the road can strip away their plans for rising in the world.

This is nothing new: *Jaques got ill while we were in together on a truck that we were paying off in forty instalments. This was in '89. We paid the deposit on the truck, started paying the instalments, and then two, three months later he got sick and couldn't drive any more. All I know is that the truck came to nothing, we lost the investment because there was no way I could keep paying alone. He died not long after, leaving nothing to his wife, because the little Jaques had saved he'd invested in the deposit on the truck. No use crying about it, we lost our money. And I lost my friend.*

The economic and social crisis that the country has been facing for years affects these drivers acutely, since they immediately feel the hit of economic downturns, fuel cost inflation, worsening infrastructure, the rise in cargo theft and the many forms of precariousness in work and social security.

I ask myself if these transformations in the fabric of the truck drivers' lives, in their imaginations, in their forms of solidarity and everyday life on the roads can help us in understanding where we've got to as a country. We didn't know at the time, but that strike would be the prologue to an election in October of that year that would be unlike any other.

—

Not so long ago, we were exposed to frequent scenes of a hospitalized president. The nation discusses his intestines. Newspapers consult specialists in hernias, hiccups, reflux and other maladies of the insides.

He likes to exhibit his scars like a war hero's medals. We watch the performance of the presidential body posing for the cameras in hospital beds, showing his scars in Facebook 'lives' and discussing his sex life at public events with the same ease with which he praises torturers and mocks the dead and the sick.

That body marks the nation with its invasive presence. However, under each of his acts of exposure, a notable absence should strike us: that of the bodies of the sick accumulating beneath his hyena's laugh. That body and its blemishes echo the image of José Millán-Astray, the Francoist butcher and founder of the Spanish Legions who arrogantly paraded his combat scars – a disfigured face, a torn-out eye, a missing arm, an almost toothless smile. He showed off these wounds as signs of the superiority of those who love the smell of battles and get off on the dead bodies of their enemies. The Francoist's mutilated body served as a living monument to the persecution of the opposition, the shutting down of universities, militarized machismo, the politics of *viva la muerte.*

For my father and the other patients I have spent time with over recent months, an understanding of the suffering of others frequently opens the road to dialogue and empathy. In the hospital's corridors, it's common for patients to start a conversation with him the moment they notice his colostomy bag or his urinary catheter, or while we wait for the next radiotherapy session. Very often they show their own scars and enumerate the different medicines they're on, the long hours they've spent waiting for yet another consultation, the highs and lows of treatment. They share tricks for tackling hospital bureaucracy and,

112

every now and then, slide along their chair, coming closer to reveal, at a whisper, how they deal with urinary incontinence, frequent diarrhoea, sexual impotence, the fear of pain and death.

Audre Lorde, in *The Cancer Journals*, a book in which she relates the everyday experience of her breast cancer treatment, speaks of the succession of patients in the hospital sharing their stories and impressions on life after mastectomy with her: 'We compared notes on nurses, exercises, and whether or not cocoa-butter retarded Black women's tendencies to keloid'. Women who crossed her path by way of becoming ill and having to cope with it, and who forged bonds with her through their doubts and worries about what it would be like to live, be loved and desire after having their breasts amputated.

In *Regarding the Pain of Others*, Susan Sontag challenges the conventional idea that images of others' suffering, like the ones that flood the news during times of armed conflicts, might be the source of emotions with some real political power. To observe others' pain, on the contrary, can act as a form of relief, as an individual emblem of awareness of the suffering of the other, a feeling of paralyzing self-congratulation.

This reasoning doesn't just apply to images but also to numbers, especially when the bodies start numbering in the thousands. After March 2020 I began obsessively checking the number of Covid victims in the country. What does it mean, as far as the world is concerned, that on 27 March 2021, 3,409 people died, or that on 12 February 2022, 879 new deaths were recorded? I felt as though I were a part of an audience watching the macabre spectacle of our insides being put on display, dumbfounded. We became increasingly numbed to the quantity of victims, which began to affect us less and less as they reached levels so enormous that they were no longer capable of telling us anything new. When the daily death toll from Covid and the official policy of letting people die reached a thousand, I realized I could not comprehend this figure. Did I know the names of one thousand individuals? Could I see myself, inverted – my life, my privileges, my vaccine, my remote working, my health plan – in the obscene amount of corpses accumulated as a result of the spectacle of Brazilian politics during the Covid pandemic? Where was I in this number? Where were my friends and my students? Where was my father?

Occupied with counting our dead, with treating our sick and administering our lives in the middle of a pandemic and the daily political horror, we still have not managed to transform these numbers into words, into narratives that supply some meaning to our individual shock and generate some potency for political action.

As I change my father's colostomy bag, I learn that the exposed intestine feels no pain.

In the maelstrom of a pandemic, we are surrounded by images and statistics of this body-country in flames. It's no easy task to recuperate the sense of urgency and responsibility when faced with all these tragedies, catalyzed by those who occupy the highest offices in the Republic.

Perhaps one step is to look elsewhere: to take our focus away from the burning bodies and towards the hands that continue to throw petrol onto the flames. I think of the gesture made by the African American poet Claudia Rankine, who in her book *Citizen: An American Lyric* manipulates the well-known and hideous photographs of lynchings in the southern United States during the first decades of the twentieth century. Rankine erases the images of the hanging bodies and keeps the rest of the scene. What strikes us in these new versions of the photographs are the crowd's enthusiastic faces, their congregated white bodies, dressed in their Sunday best. In one of them, a young man smiles as he points to the top of the tree from which, in the original photograph, two black men are seen hanging.

The power of Rankine's photomontages seems to strike at the heart of the political lives of these images: when we see the altered lynching photos, with the cruel spectacle of the re-exhibition of black corpses erased, what remains are the excited white faces, grinning, certain of their barbarous condition as good citizens.

The light always falls on the hyena's laugh.

The political and social devastation we have lived through in recent years has its origins in the long history of Brazilian authoritarianism. Destruction became the State's official policy, the official aesthetic one of coarseness, sophisticated ideas a reason for persecution. Our illness, in its most recent guise, turns places of gloom into motives for national pride: the sawmills in the middle of the forest, the torture centres, the alleyways where death squads operate, the architecture of the 'servants' bedrooms', the apartment where the husband beats his wife, the dark lanes down which trans women are beaten, the 'back rooms' in supermarkets where security guards assault poor, young black men. These become the ethical models, the aesthetic references and the libidinal motors of a new cartography of destruction.

Illegal prospecting is the model institution: an open war for resources in which the most heavily armed win and those who still retain some humanity suffer. A sociologist is yet to write a book about 'prospector ethics and the spirit of Brazilian capitalism', this monstrosity that emerges from the elective affinity between the raw experience of the frontier – the economy of constant primitive accumulation, whose lifeblood is pillaging and death – and white-collar rentierism, an affinity that reveals the deep links between the devastation of the rainforest, the reflective office buildings on Avenida Faria Lima and the palaces of the country's state capitals.

Brazil invents its own allegories with the thick material of our daily political life. In our sad fable, it was the wolf who from the highest point shouted out for all to hear: 'Look, I'm a wolf and I'm going to eat you all up.' He projects himself into every corner and destroys what could have been configured as a social body, one that we'd thought had been strengthening over time, even at a very slow pace. The wolf hates anything that reeks of society. He is nostalgic for the filthy dungeons of those other filthy times. The beast stares deep into our eyes, eats our flesh and sucks on our bones, while he rubs his belly and laughs at our attempts to name him.

Of course, the wolf and his gang did not remain in power forever. But social time is different from election time, the cycle of periodic government renewal that is the bare minimum demanded of a democracy. Pier Paolo Pasolini, alarmed at the state of culture in 1960s Italy, warned two decades after the fall of Mussolini that 'true fascism is that which has as its target the values, the souls, the languages, the gestures, the bodies of the people.' For now, the election of 2022 has thankfully opened up new political paths, but this new form of brutality will live on regardless for some time. It will continue to show its twisted face and its sharpened teeth for a long time, in our public institutions, on social networks, at family lunches, in our language, medical consultations, police stations, birthday parties, religious cults, dark alleys and highways.

VIII. JAQUES

Jaques was my companion on the road, in the bar, at parties, in fights. A friend who was only a metre and a half tall but could take on anyone.

He only ever wore short shorts and flip-flops. If there was a fight in the middle of one of those dirt roads, he'd throw down his Havaianas and challenge the other guy right there.

I remember once we were about to cross on a ferry and it was Jaques's turn to pass over, I was going after him. This was to cross the River Xingu, we were on our way to Belém. When the ferry pulled over, two trucks disembarked – only two trucks could pass at a time. And there was a big beast of a driver who got there after us and went on before me and Jaques. He skipped the queue and was saying it was his turn. This man was twice the size of Jaques.

'I don't care, I'm crossing,' this idiot said.

Jaques lost it. He said it was our turn and we were going to board the ferry. They began shouting at each other, right in each other's faces. The big guy even got to a stage where he beat his chest and said: 'I'm a real man and I'm crossing first.'

At this, Jaques threw his two Havaianas to one side and said: 'Look how short I am, I don't need to beat my chest and go on about being a real man, 'cos everyone here can see that I'm a man.' And he tripped this sucker into the scrub so that he fell over, almost burst the lanky beanpole against the floor.

And he was flailing around and kicking, desperate to kick up a fuss. Jaques said: 'Didi, don't get involved. Didi, stay back! Leave it to me, I can deal with it.' And since I don't like fighting, I just cheered him on and watched, I knew what an animal he could be.

He was such a show-off, Jaques. He had a real talent for playing tricks, drinking cachaça and making up stories.

Once we were heading to Rio Branco in Acre. At that time the transportation companies would put a white line with red letters on the yellow fabric covering the truck, to catch everyone's attention: 'Such and such a transportation coming, going here or there.' Rio Branco was another world, so far away, so they advertised the company along the journey.

So we left Jaú and headed for Acre. We went to Presidente Prudente, where the road splits for São Paulo and Mato Grosso. The city on the other side of the border is called Bataguassu. We stopped at a station, it was seven at night, we had a few cocktails. He put his little hand on his waist, one foot on his knee and the other on the floor. And the owner of the little bar asked where we were going. Jaques said, 'We're off to Belém, Pará, they're opening a branch of the Bank of Brazil and we've got stacks of brand-new, freshly printed banknotes loaded in the trailer. The rest is just new telephones and calculators.' It was all lies. We were just carrying bits and bobs, old office chairs, waste paper, wardrobes, used things the agency in São Paulo had spare to send to Rio Branco.

But there were two guys next to us who probably weren't crooks but got big ideas when they heard the truck was loaded with money. These two stole the cap from the tank of Jaques's truck and when we left they followed after us. And then the guys began honking as they passed his truck, to show him they had the cap. Jaques was no fool, he realized they were crooks out to get him.

So he just accelerated, rammed into their truck, almost flew straight over them. It was a complete mess.

I was in the truck behind, and I saw the commotion, Jaques ploughing his truck forwards and backwards, trying to ram into them. When these guys realized there was no way of stopping him, they drove ahead a hundred, a hundred and fifty kilometres. Then they stopped again and began to follow us. At that point, Jaques was really scared, all his bravado vanished.

We drove on like crazy. We stopped in Coxim, a bit ahead, where there was a highway police stand and a gas station, which was where we were going to eat and sleep.

He entered the highway police stand like a crazy person, shouting: 'Stop, thief, stop, thief!' The highway police were stunned: 'Hold on, where is this thief?' Then he explained the situation to the officer.

Night passed, day dawned. We saw no more of the thieves. Good.

So we kept going. We passed Cuiabá and went onto the dirt road. But a little further ahead, there was a sawmill with the nickname Crate. We gave each mill a nickname: Jaguar's Curve, Christ's Head, Owl's Beak... We'd just passed Crate when I saw Jaques flying down the road. It was roughly two-thirty in the afternoon and these guys had appeared again, with a pick-up. The pick-up appeared, went in front of him, so he jumped out of the truck and ran so deep into the heart of that forest that I couldn't see him any more. It took him around an hour and a half to get back.

—

A little further on there's a place called Jangada, a small village. He went into the police station to talk to an officer. 'I want an escort to accompany me for at least two days so I can get away from these bandits because we've been running from them for two days and we keep being followed.' The officer said he had no officers for an escort: 'But if you want, there's two gunslingers who'll do it; here's the address, tell them I sent you.'

The gunmen came straight away. Jaques paid for their food, paid for everything that day. And if he found the bandits, the order to the gunslingers was to kill – the officer said so. At the time there was no pretence, they killed and everyone knew it. The two guys came with a twelve-gauge shotgun. They got in the truck and came with us for the rest of the day and a bit of the night too. We slept, kept going the next day, saw nothing. After two days, Jaques paid them and got rid of them. We had lunch in that place.

But ahead there's a place called Pimenta Bueno, where Uncle Nerso used to buy wood, and he was there. And believe it or not, me and Jaques stopped there too just as it was beginning to get dark. 'Let's sleep here, I won't travel at night any more,' he said. All right then.

We stopped at the station, took a shower, sat down at the bar, he ordered a cocktail, I said, 'Cachaça please,' then we ate dinner. Uncle Nerso was there, but Jaques hadn't seen him. Nerso crept up behind him, poked him with two fingers and said, 'This is a stick-up.' Jaques fainted. He went out like a light, fell on the floor, flipping over and trembling. We shook him and shook him, until he came round. Had our drinks, chatted with Nerso, slept there... And that was the last of the thieves.

Jaques died of AIDS a while after this. You knew him a bit as a child.

I remember a little before he got ill, we were on a trip from São Luís de Maranhão. He said: 'Didi, watch out for this new disease, there's no cure for it, it's a deadly virus. They're saying it's called AIDS. Once you've got it, you don't get better.' I'd never heard of it, this was the beginning of AIDS. And he got it soon after, died a few years later.

Jaques was the devil made flesh. I know God has found a good place for him.

IX. CAB

'Do you understand? Have you ever felt the numb pain of yearning? They say there is a yearning of the mind and a yearning of the heart. They say the government is going to open up a good highway from Pirapora to Paracatú, up that way.'
— João Guimarães Rosa, *The Devil to Pay in the Backlands*

You were made in the cab of a truck.

My parents conceived me on the last night of their honeymoon trip, in the cab of a truck parked at a roadside stand near Marília, São Paulo. There is a brief note on this last night of travel in my mother's diary: 'On 3 March we stopped at one-thirty to sleep in Marília and reached Jaú at nine.'

Ever since I was I child, my parents have talked to me about this trip and how I was 'made' on the return leg. They also tell the story of the journey to friends, relatives and new acquaintances. They tell the story, laugh, and my mother says to me, 'That's why you don't like to stay in one place.'

They show photos of the trip. In one of them, they pose in front of a light blue Mercedes truck, my father's right arm over her shoulder, her hand on his waist. He's wearing shorts and a shirt open down to his belly button, she has on a lilac T-shirt, orange hotpants, her hair curled from the perm she had done for her wedding. His face is serious, she's smiling. Next to the truck, two stools and some kitchen gadgets they used to prepare meals on the road in a small gas stove. They brought a large tin full of pieces of fried meat with them from Jaú, pre-filled with pork fat to preserve the food along the journey. It's impossible to identify where the photo was taken: a dusty highway, low-lying pasture all around it, it could be anywhere between Jaú and Belém.

My father arrived in Jaú with his truck loaded with equipment that he was taking to an aluminium factory being built in Belém. They were married the next day in the Nossa Senhora Aparecida church, spent the night in the city, went to Belém together to deliver the cargo and then came back. That was the longest journey of my mother's life, a stretch my father had already done dozens of times.

This honeymoon in the cab of a truck carries strong traces of my parents' origin, their sense of belonging to a social universe in which work, leisure and the way you conceive of your country are interlinking roads, weaving a storyline out of images and words from their daily lives. To my ears, this story also has a ring of an origin myth to it, an adventure that links my life to the road in a way that is at once intimate and remote.

They dated for nine years, but my mother always says: 'If you add it all up, the courtship was less than two years, because your father was always travelling.' The yearning and the expectations for the long-awaited marriage make up the central themes of my mother's journal during that time. She worked, went to Mass and prayer groups, lived with her parents, met her closest friends on the weekend and waited for my father. While they were courting, she worked at the Camargo Correa textile factory in Jaú, as well as doing repairs from home for friends and neighbours and helping my grandmother with the housework. Before that she had worked as a cleaner and a cooking assistant for a few years in the house of a well-off Lebanese family who owned the city's biggest department store. As a child and teenager, she worked on the farm and helped to bring up her three youngest siblings. Later, while my father was recovering from his first cardiac surgery, she was a hospital porter and a cleaner at a residence for nuns.

In her diary, the declarations of longing live alongside collages of besotted couples, images my mother cut out of photo comics and love poems she copied from women's magazines of the time.

> On 11 August 1983 we booked the pre-marriage course and arranged the wedding in the church at six.

> On 28 August 1983, we had the pre-marriage course from seven-thirty to five. Then at night we went to the fair.

> We were together from ten in the morning until eleven-twenty at night. We were together for thirteen hours and twenty minutes. It was wonderful. If God wills it, we'll be married in five months' time.

> 2 October 1983, Sunday, twelve days since I saw my Love, he called me, said everything's fine and he won't be back until the twelfth or thirteenth.

As the wedding approaches, the diary records a frantic routine of activity and anxiety. There were all the invitations to send out, the wedding dress commission given to my father's seamstress cousin, the visits from relatives eager to see the wedding presents, all carefully placed on the new wedding bed and photographed next to the guests.

And then the wedding and the trip: '11 February, Didi and I married. It was a wonderful day. We were married in church at six, followed by the registry office at six-thirty, and then we had our photo taken in the garden, in our house and then we went to my mother-in-law's house, had dinner and went to see Aunt Sula. I went home to take off my clothes and then we went over to my mother-in-law's to play bingo and then we went to sleep in the chapel guesthouse. It was a wonderful night.'

My mother briefly describes each stretch of the journey in her notebook: the stopping points, the familiar faces they meet on the way, the excursions in Belém (the church, the park, the market, the café), ferry crossings and the routines of life on the road: 'Friday 17 February 1984, we unloaded the truck and spent four and a half hours on a ferry.' '18 February, I stayed in Zefa Saturday and Didi went to get his cargo and met Luis Carlos and Manezinho, we had lunch in Zefa and at night we had dinner and went to the bar to drink Coca-Cola.'

Annie Ernaux, in her vast body of work, takes on a central plot from a range of angles: the story of the girl who distances herself from her parents' class and then tries to understand them, while at the same time attempting to make sense of her own place in the world. Other writers whose biographies are similarly shaped by the story of working-class filiation have constructed their oeuvres around this fundamental tension – Tove Ditlevsen, James Baldwin, Didier Eribon, Édouard Louis, among other travellers between social classes. These are tales of betrayal, as Ernaux tells us, of an abyss between different ways of situating oneself in the world and of the fraught attempts to build bridges and create sites of convergence made from memories, places, words, tastes and feelings.

There's a common thread connecting the stories of those who have experienced the complex and unforgettable process of changing social class: over the years, we

128

feel compelled to distance ourselves from those who first showed us the world. We are forced (and force ourselves) to break free of their habits, their movements, their ways of dealing with money, the home and the body, their tastes and, above all, their words. But despite this sinuous process of deconstructing and reconstructing the self, something always insists on remaining. In Pierre Bourdieu's formula, we carry with us through the world our 'cleft habitus', a two-way bridge on the frontier between our selves and a social universe in which we live in separate places. This feeling of rupture is even more extraordinary in societies, such as Brazil, that are riven by inequality, and it certainly affects in a more profound way the subjective structure and the social ties of those who are not part of the racial group predominant in the elite – as the psychoanalyst and psychiatrist Neusa Sousa Santos exposed magisterially in her book *Becoming Black*, which analyzes the unconscious strategies and the forms of subjective suffering of black people who ascended socially in early-1980s Brazil.

This double class belonging often condenses itself into a diffuse and persistent feeling of guilt, of social and institutional alienation, an intrusive sensation of inadequacy or insufficiency, a frequent fear of 'losing everything', as well as a burden of responsibility for our parents' wellbeing – now that we are on the ascent, we cannot leave them behind.

We burst with anger when faced with those everyday scenes of injustice that make up the infernal machinery through which the elites perpetuate themselves. We bear witness to these mechanics of inequality every day, in all the new places in which we circulate, and these situations are generally understood immediately. Class migrants often have a knack for social analysis, which rarely compensates for the personal cost of inhabiting this split condition.

No one elaborated this drama of our peripheral capitalism in a more sophisticated manner than Machado de Assis, himself a frequenter of several social worlds. His novels and stories are full of characters from the Brazilian elite whose skills and achievements are at best mediocre, but who still manage to guarantee their comfortable positions at the top of a perversely unequal society which exists alongside the cynical lustre of Europeanized liberal ideas. At the bottom of the pyramid, Machado composes a rich painting of the victims of Brazilian violence, both material and symbolic: people who are free but dependent on white masters, and enslaved individuals for whom the risk of real death is compounded by the slow social death of slavery.

After my birth, my mother never kept another diary or wrote any more letters. The last entry in the diary is a note to my father, written when I was a newborn. She signs it in her name and mine. These lines are the prehistory of my writing, just as, for her, they are a sort of farewell to writing:

Dido I love you
I'm only happy when you're by my side.
Me you and our son
I love you more each passing day.
Now it's two hearts that love you, mine and our son's
Dido, remember this someone who loves you so much
and will always be waiting for you
Dirce – and the fruit of our
Love our son

I'm struck by a line of Ernaux's where she talks about her mother – the picture it paints is strangely familiar to me: 'I was both certain of her love for me and aware of one blatant injustice: she spent all day selling milk and potatoes so that I could sit in a lecture hall and learn about Plato.' The story of parents and children who had radically different educational trajectories is always cut through by silence and avoidance, since significant parts of our day-to-day reality – our work, our reading, our tastes and our expenditures – are hard to translate into our parents' universe.

One day, while explaining to my father that for my PhD I was studying the politics around architecture and popular housing, he demanded in no uncertain terms: *When you speak to them, tell them poor people deserve bigger houses.*

In academic discourse, a statement like this would be dissected in endless discussions on the epistemology of the 'speech' of the researcher (who should speak to power?), on the public and private decision makers responsible for housing policy (who are the actors?) and on the historical and political construction of ideas like 'the dream of owning your own home' (the perennial debate surrounding the inclusion of the poorest people into society via the route of consumption).

None of this is spurious. My academic work is devoted to such questions and I take them very seriously. But I recognize that it's often enough to simply tell them that poor people deserve bigger houses – and we all know who 'they' are.

X. WHAT IS MINE

'Pessimism was sometimes "organized" to the point
of producing, by its very performance, the intermittent flash and hope of fireflies. A flash to make words
appear freely, at a time when words seemed taken
captive by a situation with no way out.'
—— Georges-Didi Huberman

*I'm playing truco, but I've got no more cards in my hand. I'm
bluffing. And I'm winning, for now.*

Since the cancer diagnosis, he has been calculating
how much longer he will be able to keep bluffing: most of
the time, he concludes that he has two years left. On more
optimistic days, this number increases to three or four.
Or he discreetly contracts the figure, as with the words he
chose to wish me a happy new year at the start of 2022: *I'm
happy to be starting the year with you.*

My father's speech, like that of every old man, is populated by ruins and the dead. There are stretches of road that
have been engulfed by forest, a garage that has become an
orthodontic consultancy, forests of his childhood that are
now sugar cane plantations, rivers once brimming with
fish now filled with sewage. His mother and his father
are dead, many of his siblings and friends already gone.
His own language acknowledges this decomposition: his
speech is woven from the confusion of verbal tenses, in
the coexistence of words, some new and others corroded
by time, in frequent nostalgic nods to fabulation as the
antidote to memory lapses.

In our conversations, when he finishes telling some story about life on the roads, he often concludes: *such was life.*
The tense of this phrase, that enigmatic past, multiplies

the meanings of the word 'life'. In the first meaning, the life referred to is the one in which the body and the work in the truck were both in their early days – and that one is gone. Or else, the life being referred to is more expansive and still endures; but it's likely it will be over soon, and that's why he resorts to the preterite as an announcement, a tragic recognition and a nod of solidarity with our coming mourning, a mourning that will be just ours, and not his – because we all know that such is life.

The biological mutation my father's body has undergone over recent months is accompanied by other metamorphoses.

Illness heralds a new terrain of sensations. He learns to navigate a complex phenomenology of cancer: multiple boxes and jars of medicine, bags, patches, materials of varying viscosity, substances which go in and out of the body to keep it functioning. Audre Lorde tells us that each amputation is 'a physical and psychic reality that must be integrated into a new sense of self', and I believe that the same can be said about the addition of these new artificial members which become part of the body – colostomy bags, drains, nappies, catheters, bands, walkers, Holter monitors, dressings and chemical grafts which replace degraded physiological processes.

These paraphernalia are joined by a vast documental cartography, the reams of medical requests, prescriptions, tickets, reports, exams, receipts, vaccination cards, paper wristbands and protocols.

And a chorus of moans, persistent buzzing from the queue ticketing system display, chairs being dragged, sentences repeated thousands of times – 'The doctor isn't here yet', 'You'll have to be patient, sir', 'You'll have to take another ticket', 'What medicines are you taking?', 'All you can do is wait', 'You'll have to come back tomorrow'. A universe of expressions of support, both appropriate and inappropriate – 'Everything will be OK', 'You need to have faith', 'You're strong'.

A public archive of similar cases, selectively transmitted to the sick patient so that only the success stories reach him.

The exhausting regime of waiting, the slow passing of hours during surgery and radiotherapy days, the months between one consultation and another. The calendar of changing colostomy bags and urinary drains. The many minutes of agony before being seen when my father had been unable to urinate for forty-eight hours and felt like he was exploding from the inside.

An ecology of out-of-place body odours and fluids, some pretty well known, others new. The smells of chemical products for deep cleaning, hospital smells, smells of materials that spill out of the new bags and their imperfect seals, and a new odour we are learning to identify: the smell of the tumour and its viscous materials.

An immense forest of different forms of knowledge and silences: procedures are questioned, put forth, withheld, contrasted, badly explained, not understood, forgotten. We begin to live with an enigmatic system of authorities in dispute, different powers connected like links in a chain we cannot apprehend.

Most doctors speak too quickly, too quietly, using too many technical terms. My father's hearing is getting worse, and the masks imposed by the pandemic mean he understands almost nothing the doctors say. My brother and I get used to acting as amplifiers and translators of these messages, sentence by sentence (nurses, on the other hand, always raise their voices when they realize he can't hear).

In the centre of this little bubble, my father informs us that we are the ones who will take decisions about his treatment: *I'll do whatever you and João think is best.*

For the community around the patient, the interpretation of indexes becomes an incessant routine. Illness is a forest of signs, a stage for the continuous reading of sensations, colours, smells, volumes, temperatures, reports, pains and consistencies that may mean something or may mean nothing, may or may not be symptoms, may or may not make sense – and in this case, making sense means witnessing the humours of cancer.

Changes in the colour of faeces herald a possible worsening of the condition, a strange pain in the back might be a sign of metastasis or simply be the effect of advancing age, difficulty urinating may or may not signal that the tumour has reached the prostate, and we're not sure if weight loss is good or bad news.

It's easy to cross the border between careful attention and diagnostic paranoia. When should we stop attributing meaning to body signals? We become obsessive interpreters of a body-text in a constant state of change, an open work which always demands another reading, a new choice of words which seal off this overflow of pains, sounds, fluids, smells, colours and sensations we observe either directly or through the medium of the patient's words.

My father is part of this community of readers. He's the only one with access to his body's various manifestations, its deep layers, unknown to the rest of us. As the dying Ilyich feels: 'He suffered ever the same unceasing agonies and, in his loneliness, pondered always on the same insoluble question: "What is this?"' The patient lives the reality of their illness like a shipwreck.

We are terribly poor when it comes to our vocabulary of illness. Virginia Woolf, an exuberant citizen of the world of health complaints and language, wrote of how English lacked the means to address being ill – surprising, given the centrality of illness to the human experience:

> English, which can express the thoughts of Hamlet and the tragedy of Lear, has no words for the shiver and the headache ... The merest schoolgirl, when she falls in love, has Shakespeare, Donne, Keats to speak her mind for her; but let a sufferer try to describe a pain in his head to a doctor and language at once runs dry.

In hospital, when faced with a body that suffers in three dimensions, doctors repeat the miserably linear question: 'How would you rate the pain from zero to ten?' The patient's condition is translated into the strange language of imaging tests, laboratory tests, tumour marker measurements, infrequent probings, faltering attempts at touch.

With time, listening to him and becoming more familiar with his expressions, I start to learn the limits of the language we use to surround that experience with meaning: cancer as a fight; cancer as a stage towards the cure; cancer as a possible cause of death; cancer as an unspeakable evil; cancer as a part of everyday life. All these forms of speech that are culturally imposed and that we must make use of when necessary are at once partially true and pathetically impoverished.

Across the table sits the oncologist, who rarely looks at my father. He spends nearly the entire consultation staring at his computer screen, adding words to the file to which we have no access. Doctors in different specialities argue amongst themselves through the opaque means of these electronic documents: an oncologist who recommends surgery, a surgeon who refuses to operate on account of the risk to the heart, a second surgeon who proposes surgery in a region far away from the original tumour, a cardiologist who disagrees with the first surgeon, a second oncologist who does not understand the decisions of the first one, a third surgeon who disagrees with all the others.

Specialists only communicate by means of those medical files which they hurriedly consult when the patient is in front of them, and dozens of other patients are waiting to be seen.

We're governed by the protocols that orchestrate the movement of bodies and papers. In his account of being an oncological patient, Jean-Claude Bernardet tells us:

> They were the doctors of my cancer ... protocol doctors ... One feature of this robotic facet is to keep the client's body at a distance. Touching is the exception, everything is mediated by images, exams and reports. Hand-shaking is a mere formality.

At times, I feel that some of the doctors are first and foremost guardians of these protocols, certainly more than they are doctors of the cancer itself or of my father.

The territory of my father's body is divided into different branches, commanded by heart specialists, gut experts, urethra doctors, tamers of cancer cells. With their

138

instruments, they set out to explore the body, establishing the territories under their jurisdiction, plots where they can plant their speciality's flag, like colonial geographers drawing borders on a map of the empire.

With each journey to a different hospital department, this dismembering of my father is further entrenched, a gradual process that always brings to my mind the charts of cows hanging on the walls of butcher's shop, in which each part of the animal is circumscribed and named.

A sick body asks to be seen in its totality, but in reality hears only partial answers. Even so, he continues in spite of his fragile internal borders: my father suffers as a whole.

For decades, psychoanalysis has taught us that we are not born whole. We arrive in the world pulverized by a sea of sensations, body parts, noises and fluids which, through an imaginary process, begin to take on a semblance of unity. This ontological fiction, the idea that we are whole, may be one of the most ancient foundational stones of western civilization – the belief that we have physical and psychic frontiers that separate us from the world and from others, which allow some hope of continuity over our history and a sense of coherence and autonomy in our subjective reality. Without this illusion, we are launched into the infernal abyss of not being able to differentiate between ourselves and the world. Hence our typical terror of everything that threatens to tear us apart, be that materially or in terms of the image we have of ourselves. The body with no frontiers or unity is what defines the anguish at the centre of madness, or the political utopias of networked bodies and emotions typical of a contemporary criticism of identity, oneness, integration.

My father's body, however, fragmented by medical

knowledge, is not the shattered body of the psychotic or one of Donna Haraway or Gilles Deleuze's somatic alliances: it is primarily the result of an operation of power which compartmentalizes in order to see, control, treat and, it is hoped, cure. Its resistance is innocently modern: here exists a person, a man with a name and a history, a living being that suffers and needs care, a subject who loves and fears, a citizen with rights, a creature who continues to feed the fiction of being whole, who asserts his totality beyond the parts established by medical knowledge.

If my father were a lawyer, engineer or entrepreneur, if he had a PhD like me, would he have a body beyond the sum of its parts? Would he still be able to sustain the essential illusion of being one?

Undeniably, the business of compartmentalizing the patient is a chapter in the history of medicine that has been fundamental for allowing each of its specialities to advance. But this logic is political too: through its operation, in the day-to-day running of clinics and hospitals, it unveils a social structure in which members of the working class are subordinated to the production line of immense hospitals and their shortfalls, to the bureaucratic violence that permeates the circulation of these workers' bodies through the corridors and rooms of these immense Kafkaesque machines.

Questions from the patient or their companions are almost always taken as a sign of disrespect towards the medical authority. More than once, we were subjected to risible scenes of rudeness or contempt that were almost as violent as the illness being combatted.

One of the doctors shouts at my brother, accusing him of wanting answers for everything. He then says that at this moment what he recommends is 'fasting and prayer'.

140

My mother laments that there's nothing to be done, since we depend on them.

My father: *It seems like whenever we ask questions, they treat us worse.*

I'm an ecological disaster, he jokes, referring to the sticky organic matter that bulges in his geriatric nappies. We laugh together at the way he refers to the small reserve of waste that forms there, a mixture made of biological matter that has gone the wrong way, the disorder of things, this promiscuous cohabitation of urine, sweat and secretions from his tumour in contact with the skin of his thigh and buttocks, occupying the furrows of my father's flaccid skin.

We grow accustomed to living alongside a body that hurts and no longer moves with ease. Gradually, we learn a new choreography of care. It's Carolina, a nursing assistant, who teaches me how to clean and change the colostomy bag while I help my father to wash for the first time. Carolina did this with discreet sympathy and the meticulous care of a Japanese artisan. In that hospital bathroom, my father was going through one of his most fragile moments, and I wondered if I would exit that bathroom into a new reality – a life in which I would have to play the part of carer to a sick father.

—

When inside and outside inevitably meet, someone has to clean up. Most days, this someone is him. But it's also often me, my brother or my mother, especially after surgery, when his movement remains reduced for days, sometimes weeks.

Philip Roth captured this in some of his best lines, when

describing encountering his sick father's excrement:

> You clean up your father's shit because it has to be cleaned up, but in the aftermath of cleaning it up, everything that's there to feel is felt as it never was before ... [O]nce you sidestep disgust and ignore nausea and plunge past those phobias that are fortified like taboos, there's an awful lot of life to cherish ... There was my patrimony: not the money, not the tefillin, not the shaving mug, but the shit.

My patrimony is my father's words – the words of those stories from my childhood and the ones I have heard over these last few years, as I helped to care for his fragile body.

He fondly remembers working on the Mogi-Bertioga highway, according to him one of the most beautiful landscapes he ever encountered. He is impressed by the human capacity to cut into hills, perforate rocks, blow up immense portions of the mountains in order to design the sinuous highway. And he's delighted by the view of the sea, down there, a few kilometres away. *I worked there for years, but the truck driver's life was the life of the road, and in all those years I never once put my feet in the sea.*

What kind of way of seeing a country is this, through its asphalt banks, through its passing places? He has barely been to any of the country's state capitals, merely skirted around them in his truck. Truck drivers' geography is one of connections, and their environments are those that in other people's stories are transitory and lacking in importance. Listening to him, I force myself to understand to what extent there is a kernel of truth in that life of always being on the move. It's no coincidence that 'road' is such an overused metaphor, so often employed as an artifice for us to refer to a long process of learning, an existential crossing, a process of slow transformation – in other words, life. Very often, it's on the road to Damascus – and not in Damascus – that we learn to see in other ways.

Only I can face up to what is mine.

He was talking about the cancer and its destructive impulse. But the shadow of death was not merely the hidden theme of that utterance, but also the place from which he uttered it. Walter Benjamin tells us that '[d]eath is the sanction of everything the storyteller can tell. He has borrowed his authority from death.' Rereading these words my father spoke on one of the most critical days in his treatment, I reflect that the almost complete absence of written records and images of his life on the road was also a guarantee of his autonomy, then and now, as a truck driver and storyteller. The freedom to live and tell stories, to choose what to share with me, to choose which words he would direct to anyone who asked him about his life. In this condition, only he could face his story and fully understand exactly what it was that was his.

He was now taking up his place as a storyteller and facing it with the same courage with which he faced up to his most difficult health problems and the artillery of medical procedures.

—

After one operation, when he woke up with his mouth still limp and his speech slurred by the anaesthesia, he said proudly: *I can take on a doctor in a knife fight.*

After each of his operations, he always asks the surgeon the same three questions: *When can I drive again? When can I drink beer? And have a barbecue?*

In April 2022, after months of impasse in his treatment and a range of misunderstandings between the doctors who had cared for him so far, we decide to get an opinion from a new oncologist. He analyzes all the tests, listens to my story and recommends a consultation with a gastric surgeon that same day. The two separately describe the same scenario of the disease progressing unless the tumour is removed immediately. These scenes of horror are described with professionalism but also with an honesty so graphic I am unable to share them with my parents and brother in full detail.

'Unless the cardiologist guarantees that he will definitely die on the operating table, I will operate on your father,' the new surgeon says. The cardiologist alerts us to the risks but believes that his heart will manage.

In May, the gastric surgeon removes the tumour and a large part of the colon, as well as a small part of the prostate where a bowel loop was stuck. There are no signs of a tumour outside the intestine. After the surgery, the doctor asks if I want to see a photograph of the 'piece' that was removed. I do. On his mobile phone screen, I see for the first time that reddish-brown mass that was obstructing the final portion of his intestine and crossing the organ wall. The tumour looked both diabolical and ridiculous, in equal measure. He also shows my father the image and describes each of the parts: this is the tumour, this is the portion of the intestine that went up to the rebuilt colostomy, and beneath this the anus, which was also amputated.

Well, doctor, I guess that means no more shitting myself!

Around this time, he mentions on the phone that from now on he will live for us – me, my brother, my mother. Of course, there is a nod to his finitude in this comment. But there is also an affirmation of his role in life, something like: 'Look: I matter, I'm still here.'

And he is. As a truck driver, my father learnt to cook, a rare thing among men of his generation. The long distances between restaurants and the need to economize with food meant he had to cook on the roadside, using a gas stove and a few bits of apparatus. He became an exquisite cook, over the years developing a vast menu of his own. Meat is his speciality. Few can barbecue like my father. He's friends with his favourite butcher, the only one in the city he still admires, after years of arguing and severing relations with all the others – he swears that none of them knew how to do the cuts in the right way, that they were swindlers, that their service lacked the appropriate care and attention.

My favourite dish is the polenta he gets exactly right, just on the soft side, with chicken broth and a fried egg on top, its yolk perfectly soft. But he's also renowned among friends and relatives for his *arroz carreteiro*, his roast chicken with chips and Calabrian sausage, his beer-marinated tri-tip, the ox tongue in red sauce, and a *feijoada* to die for.

To this day, whenever we speak on the phone, he makes a point of asking if I've eaten. He often says: *My greatest fear is you going hungry.*

In recent years, he's devoted himself to making lunch-boxes for his two sons, which we bring with us when we visit Jaú. On top of each lunchbox he has put a label describing the dish: *minsmeat, styu, ris, sosige.* The words come like that, written the way he hears them. This is the art of his orthography, as personal and true as the food he prepares.

I left a good number of my books in Jaú while I was doing my PhD in the United States. My father built a bookcase to store them. As well as making a piece of furniture, he came up with a joke: whenever I visited, he would say he'd read a new shelf of books and that soon he would have read them all. Before this, when he had visited my brother and me in our university halls of residence, he liked to say that students on campus looked at him and said, *Look at that old professor over there*, or, *They've invited me to come and give a lecture on trucks.* When I say I'm writing an academic article or preparing a class, he always says, *OK, any questions, just ask, I'll set you straight.*

On our recent trips to hospital, I have also learnt to play at passing in his world. I say I miss my friends from the road and the sunrise on the Mogi-Bertioga highway. I mention that, when I worked in Mr Ítalo's garage, I made a gate that lasted more than sixty years, and that I missed drinking cachaça in Dona Iolanda's bar on the corner. And how I wish I could load my truck onto a ferry on the Rio Negro, see the *pororoca* again, battle through mudholes on those dirt roads, see the forests in the north of the country again.

After a month recuperating in São Paulo, my parents returned to Jaú in June 2022. The treatment continues there.

Recently, he bought some new, more resistant containers for making the lunchboxes. *That way they'll last longer and I can still do a lot of cooking for you.*

When I visited them shortly after the operation, we sat

in the yard after dinner. On warm nights, he likes to rest there in a rocking chair.

'You like sitting here, don't you, Dad? Taking in the air and thinking about life?'

Thinking about life, eh?... Life is life, there's not much to think about.

Sources

Roland Barthes, *Sade, Fourier, Loyola*, XVII, tr. Richard Miller (New York: Farrar, Straus & Giroux, 1974).

Barthes, *The Preparation of the Novel*, tr. Kate Briggs (New York: Columbia University Press, 2010).

Georges Didi-Huberman, *Survival of the Fireflies*, tr. Lia Swope Mitchell (Minneapolis: University of Minnesota Press, 2018).

Tove Ditlevsen, *Childhood, Youth, Dependency*, tr. Tina Nunnally (London: Penguin, 2020).

Didier Eribon, *Returning to Reims*, tr. Michael Lucey (London: Penguin, 2019).

Annie Ernaux, *A Woman's Story*, tr. Tanya Leslie (London: Fitzcarraldo Editions, 2024).

João Guimarães Rosa, *The Devil to Pay in the Backlands*, tr. James L. Taylor and Harriet De Onís (New York: Alfred A. Knopf, 1963).

Guimarães Rosa, *The Third Bank of the River and other stories*, tr. William L. Grossman (New York: Alfred A. Knopf, 1968) .

Audre Lorde, *The Cancer Journals* (London: Penguin Classics, 2020).

Siddhartha Mukherjee, *The Emperor of All Maladies* (London: 4th Estate, 2011).

Graciliano Ramos, *Linhas tortas* (Rio de Janeiro: Record, 2005).

Philip Roth, *Patrimony* (New York: Simon & Schuster, 1991).

Maria Stepanova, *In Memory of Memory*, tr. Sasha Dugdale (London: Fitzcarraldo Editions, 2021).

Virginia Woolf, *On Being Ill* (Middletown, CT: Paris Press, 2012).

Acknowledgements

To Rita, my first-rate editor who supported this project from the very beginning, and all the team at Fósforo.

To Michele, Marcela, Felipe and Helena, for their generous words and eyes.

To Ana, my partner on the crossing.

To Caio, Fred, Lívia and Mathias, companions in other inventions.

To Santiago, my cat and writing companion.

To my mother and brother, immense gratitude.

To my father, for everything I've said and much more besides.

Fitzcarraldo Editions
8-12 Creekside
London, SE8 3DX
Great Britain

ISBN 978-1-80427-085-1

Design by Ray O'Meara
Typeset in Fitzcarraldo
Printed and bound by TJ Books Limited

fitzcarraldoeditions.com

Fitzcarraldo Editions